CHARITY IN CHESHIRE

From Award winning Author
T N TRAYNOR

My thanks go to Nigel who tirelessly, without pay, helps to check my books over for the many errors I produce. Nigel you are the best muse any author could ask for, and I am very grateful for you!

Please note that US English has been used throughout.

T. N. Traynor
Publishing

Book cover by Deranged Doctor Designs
https://www.derangeddoctordesign.com

Index

T N TRAYNOR

Women of Courage

Book Three

Chapter 1

I DON'T THINK HOME IS A PLACE. It's more a sense of being and belonging. Possessions don't create the abode where I dream of dwelling anyway, which is funny really considering where I live. No, for me, home is the inner acceptance of being in the right place, at the right time, and hopefully surrounded by the right people.

So I'm really not being glib when I say *most emphatically* that diamonds are most *definitely* not a girl's best friend. Nor are money, fancy clothes or mansions. I would swap it all for friendship, someone to confide in, share my woes with, and maybe give and receive hugs now and again. Oh, how I miss being held. Somehow, over the years I seem to have lost everyone I considered a true friend, well except for Nana of course. When Nana squeezes me tight, all sorts of happiness bubble inside me. I used to blame Roland for the loss of my friends: his habit and bombastic ways are hard to tolerate for normal everyday people. But I've come to the conclusion that I am the sum of my own decisions. Does that mean I am finally growing up?

Don't get me wrong, I am not a poor little rich girl. Far from it, I'm very aware of how lucky I am, and what luxury I live in. It's just I feel empty inside. Lonely, I guess. Of course, there are a multitude of offers to do lunch, and a plethora of invitations to help with this or that charity event. I could even go to a dinner party every night of the year if I so wished, which of course I don't.

My immaculate, extremely still, reflection seems to have something she wants to say. She doesn't speak of course, captured behind the cold, hard glass of an ornate full length mirror. An echo of me, caught in a world I don't recognize with little understanding of how I got here, or to be more accurate, why I don't leave. Beauty and elegance reflect back at me. Who are you, and where have *I* gone? *When* did I go? There's no response from lifeless eyes that gaze back at me. They're what? Warning? Pitiful? Accusing?

"You ready yet, Charity? Not like you to be late for anything."

It's hard to draw my attention away from the stranger in the mirror. The silver full-length Dior haute couture gown clings to my thin frame. When did I become a size eight? It doesn't suit me, I look gaunt. 'Chic' the papers call me, but I know better, 'cliché' is more like it.

I flick my velvety, kohl-lined eyes to the side. My china-doll expressionless face tilts slightly, as I look my husband up and down. Roland is still dashing, and his Paris-designed suit will be the envy of all and the talk of celeb gossip tomorrow. At six feet two inches, he towers over my small five feet two frame; I used to love that about him. Ours had been a whirlwind romance, the stuff of dreams. Back then I'd had no idea of his privileged background. We'd simply done the same stuff as all the other students, nights in the pub, walking hand-in-hand by the river and lots of dancing. He'd always made me feel safe and petite when he wrapped his arms around me. When was the last time he'd done that?

He finishes tying his made-to-order Venetian, silver mask around his head. Peeking through, his baby blue eyes are misted over and slightly bloodshot.

Air escapes my lips with a steam-cooker hiss, while I concentrate on reining in my disappointment. He's hit the coke already. Fun party this is going to be. "I'll be down in a minute, you go ahead. I'll catch you up."

Roland finishes adjusting his bow tie and comes over. He leans down and kisses the top of my head. I'm reminded of a father's affection. "You look stunning as usual. Those diamonds suit you so well. I'm glad you changed your mind and put them on."

Anything to keep the peace. "I find them very heavy, but for you…"

"That's my girl. See you downstairs. Don't be long. This whole shebang is for you after all." Roland sniffs as he leaves the master bedroom. A shudder crawls along my back as I cringe. I can't stand that sound. It's a sound that has driven me crazy for the last four years. Well, to be honest, there's not much left about Roland that doesn't drive me crazy these days.

I reach over and pick up the white faux fur wrap off the chair, pulling it around my bare shoulders. It hides the hideous necklace perfectly. I almost crack a smile. In my hair sits a delicate diamond and pearl head-piece which, with the matching drop earrings, would have been enough for me. The cascading necklace lying so coldly upon my décolletage is just over-the-top flamboyant, but that's Roland for you. He always loves to perform. Throwing this birthday masquerade ball for me is more about showing off than expressing love.

Tightening my black-lace mask into place I lean forward and squint at the mirror. "Who *are* you, and where have *I* gone?"

Hazel eyes glisten back at me, the black mask making them appear to pop. Those I recognize, albeit their sparkle has diminished. My heart-shaped lips glisten with deep pink gloss, but they don't open to answer me.

I straighten, sucking in breath like I'm preparing for a deep-sea dive. Suddenly, I throw my arms wide, tilt my chin upwards. A slight bend of my right knee sends my hip askew. "Let's get this party started," I sing to the empty room, in full Shirley Bassey imitation. With a wink at my alien reflection, I scoop up the side of my dress and sashay out of the room, *almost* like a woman in full control.

Nearly all the rich and famous from Cheshire are here. Roland knows just who to invite, and who to 'forget' to invite. Our mansion might not be the biggest in Alderley Edge, but it boasts stunning gardens that spread out around the house like layers on a tiered skirt. The main marquee is stunning, as are the walkways that have been set up to take you from one marquee to another. Sparkling, white fairy-lights adorn every pole and edge of the tents and walkways, inter-woven into garlands of white roses. Everywhere is decorated in white, creating an illusion of a Winter Wonderland. Years ago, I would have been in awe of the fairy-tale beauty.

A band plays in the main tent. The music rocks so loud that every house in the neighborhood could go into their gardens and party along. Brash, that's Roland again. He'd insisted that speakers be put all over the house and garden so that wherever you are, you can dance.

With heaters throwing out a glowing heat every few yards, it doesn't matter that the ball is outside, despite it being December the 6th. Immaculate, good-looking, waiters and waitresses carry an overabundance of food and drink around so that guests needn't bother themselves with fetching it. The noise is uncomfortably loud. I move with practiced grace through the main marquee, greeting and exchanging brief repartee with as many people as possible, trying hard not to shout to be heard. They definitely have to shout at me though, and for the hundredth time I make a mental note to get my hearing checked out. There is something about asking stars to repeat themselves that is extremely embarrassing. Like I'm a fraud amongst the rich and famous which I guess I am, as I only married into it.

By eleven-thirty, a mannequin probably has more expression on their plastic face than I can muster on mine. The last few years of dealing with Roland's 'habit' and his string of affairs has just about left me dead inside. Plus, something has happened to me today, although I'm not completely sure what it was yet. Maybe it's to do with the fact that I've turned twenty-eight? Or maybe, that Roland has bought me a diamond necklace I detest, and I'm irritated because after seven years of marriage he obviously *still* has no idea what I like?

"Drink, Miss?"

Momentarily my blurred vision clears as I focus on the waitress in front of me. I force yet another smile.

"Thank you." I lift the flute of Champagne and the waitress makes to move away. Before she can fully turn, I ask her a question. "Have you seen my husband?"

The waitress's face is instantly flushed. "No, Miss. Sorry." Before I can ask anything else she shoots off into the crowd, her tray of glasses sparkling, and perfectly stable despite the haste.

At midnight, the cake will be brought out and I will be forced to appear happy, as these would-be-friends who are in reality nothing more than strangers will sing happy birthday. Maybe I could feign illness and go to bed early? It seems like the best option, I just need to find Roland and let him know. Smiling and nodding at people, I make my way out of the marquee and into the house.

I pause in the hallway, wondering which way to go. Just then, our housekeeper, Judith, comes out of the kitchen carrying a large knife tied with multiple ribbons that will be used to cut the cake.

"You're still here Judith! Please go home. You've been working since eight this morning."

Judith gives a weary smile. "I'm just waiting to see you cut the cake, and then I'll be off." The housekeeper might be an employee, but she is actually one of the few people I hold in my affections. Judith and my Nana Dotty are my only two confidants. I don't know where I would be without either of them. Judith has been a godsend since arriving at the house nearly four years ago. The old staff had looked down their noses at me until I could take it no more and told Roland it was the staff or me. He had begrudgingly let them go, and given a large payment to all three of them. Afterwards, I had taken much delight in hiring a new housekeeper and two gardeners. They had become 'mine' and were without exception respectful towards me. The relationship between lady of the house and housekeeper had soon turned out to be something more to me than employer and employee.

"Do you know where Roland is?"

Judith's eyes flick towards the stairs before she lowers them quickly. "I haven't seen him for a while," she answers. But I'd seen that furtive look, and dread slams down upon me, making my weight of depression heavier.

Without a word I hand Judith my glass, pick up my dress on both sides, kick off my four inch high heels, and start running up the stairs. He wouldn't be in our bed, not even Roland would do that. So at the top of the stairs I veer right towards the guest wing. My heart's pounding, like nails hammering into my pulmonary valve, tightening muscles, loss of breath.

He wouldn't do this to me again? Not on my birthday, surely? I put my hand on the door to the first bedroom. Do I *really* want to do this? Do I *really* want to know? Maybe it would be best to just return to the party? What difference would it make? Would I leave him *this* time? I've just about convinced myself that I don't want to know, when I hear Roland moaning. Anger flushes away my need to hide from pain. I turn the handle and fling open the door. My life's a flippin' cliché.

He doesn't even stop what he's doing to look at me.

Disrespect! Imitating Marilyn Monroe, I start singing. "Happy birthday to me, happy birthday to me…" Roland finally grunts and rolls off the bleached blonde. She at least has the decency to look embarrassed as she pulls the sheet up to her chin.

For goodness' sake, she only looks sixteen! "I'm going to Nana's. When I come back, we'll be discussing divorce."

11

With that I spin around and charge to my bedroom so I can change, and get out of here as soon as possible. No need to call for a taxi as we have a pile of chauffeurs downstairs waiting to take guests home.

I've just finished changing into jeans and a jumper when Roland comes staggering in. He tries to grab me in a hug. He's crying and mumbling. I push him away, and he falls back onto the bed. For a moment we stare at each other. A 'whoosh' of good-history passes between us, moments when we'd been happy and in love. The silence says so much. Unfortunately, Roland breaks the moment.

"Please don't leave. You know these women don't mean anything to me."

"Oh, for crying out loud will you grow up, and stop lying to yourself. The reason you're hell-bent on destroying yourself is because you're a coke addict. Well I've had enough. I can't fix you, God knows I've tried."

I pull a coat out of the wardrobe, pick up my everyday handbag, and start across the room.

"But I love you…"

I stop and turn around. "No you don't, and you haven't for a long time. I'll be back on Monday morning to pick up some things. I'll be calling Shardlys, so you'll have to go somewhere else for a lawyer."

Judith is waiting at the bottom of the stairs. "I've asked Tina to announce that you're not feeling well, and I've got Luke waiting at the kitchen door for you."

Gratitude washes over me, bringing me close to tears. Tina is the event planner and could be trusted to be tactful, and Luke is my favorite chauffeur. I grab Judith in a tight, brief embrace, but as tears threaten to flood I quickly let her go.

Luke is standing holding the limousine door open. He gives me a brief nod before I dive in. Once the engine's started, Luke looks at me through the driver's mirror.

"Holmes Chapel, please Luke. Dotty's house."

Chapter 2

LAST NIGHT I'D LET MYSELF IN QUIETLY through the back door, and tiptoed to my bedroom.

Now, light dances through the gap in the curtains as I listen to Dotty moving about downstairs. I don't feel like facing her and telling her why I'm here, yet again, so I can't help moaning as I hear her coming up the stairs. I feel like I am ten again, and pull the duvet up under my chin. I should have realized she would know I was here; eighty-eight she may be, but she's still bright as a button. Her serious face, lips pursed tight, does nothing to hide the love and affection in her eyes. She puts a cup of tea on the bedside cabinet, then leans down to drop a kiss on my forehead before sitting on the bed.

Nana Dotty is the epitome of perfect Granny-hood, one whose hugs and smiles can carry you through any storm. Her salt-and-pepper hair is tied in a bun at the back of her head. Her smiling eyes are surrounded by laughter lines. Her crinkled hands are soft but firm as they hold mine. If I hadn't been in this position too many times to count, I would be crying now from the relief of knowing there is at least one person in the world who never changes, one who always loves me, no matter what.

"Have your tea, my dear. Then come downstairs and tell me all about it."

"Thanks Nana."

Her all-knowing eyes bore into mine with understanding sympathy. She pats my hand and leaves me to my tea and gloomy thoughts.

Sitting up, packed with feather pillows behind me, I cradle my cup as I try to stem the torrent of thoughts that jostle for pole position within my over active mind. I can't believe he's done it to me again... no wait, yes of course I can believe he's done it again. What I can't understand is why I'm still married to him. Do I still love him? Maybe I cling to the hope that one day he'll find me enough? Obviously, I've failed our marriage. I've not been able to make him happy. I couldn't join in his lifestyle, nor could I pull him into mine. I couldn't even give him a child. No heir for his vast empire. Just what purpose could I have in his life if I can't even do that? No wonder he plays around.

"Stop feeling sorry for yourself, and get your skinny bones down here!"

I can't help laughing. Nana knows me too well. I hear her tutting to herself as she returns to the kitchen. Out of bed I pull on the fluffy dressing gown that's always on the hook on the back of the door ready for my visits, and then I head downstairs.

"Would you like some crumpets?"

"No thanks, Nana."

We automatically sit next to each other at the small round kitchen table with our backs to the wall so we can look out of the glass door into the garden. Dotty loves birds, and not far from the kitchen door is a whole array of bird feeders enticing feathery friends to come to the garden. Two robins are pecking at the winter-hardened grass, whilst blue tits and sparrows jostle for prime positions on the feeders. Three circular water baths in various heights cluster beneath the feeders, offering the birds a place to bathe and drink. For a moment we sit in comfortable silence, allowing the view to soak in and calm our spirits.

"Another woman again?" Dotty isn't one for beating around the bush.

I nod. That's easier than verbalizing his adultery.

Dotty holds her mug in both hands, squints into the garden and "Mm's."

I wait for the 'what are you doing with your life speech.' But after two minutes of silence I can't stand it anymore and blurt out. "I told him I'm filing for divorce."

"Well, that would be nice."

"Nice? What do you mean nice? He's cheating on me again. I'd hardly call it nice."

Dotty pushes her chair back a bit, so we can sit and face each other. "It would be nice if you actually woke up. It would be even better if you'd face the fact that you can't change him, you can only change you. If you should find the courage from somewhere to actually divorce him, I think you might even discover that you can stand on your own feet and design your own life. Now, *that* would be nice."

I don't know what to say. Unfortunately, we've had this discussion several times already, and I can sense that she doesn't think this time will be any different to the others. "He bought me a huge diamond necklace for my birthday."

"Lucky you." The words are heavily sarcastic. Dotty is one of those people who believe you don't need much to live on to be happy. It had taken me months to persuade her to let Roland buy this house for her five years ago. In the end it had been the combination of her old house needing a new roof and this house being right opposite the Methodist Church that had finally won her round.

I can't help rolling my eyes.

"None of that cheek," Dotty says, playfully punching my arm.

"You know I don't like over-the-top jewelry, Nana. It's really hideous. I wore my wrap all night just to hide it."

"I take it that didn't go well."

"He didn't even notice."

We're quiet for a moment as I try to verbalize that even though I've said it before, *this time* it really is time to leave.

"The necklace was the last straw, well that and the fact he had sex with some bimbo in our house right under my nose."

Dotty doesn't say anything, just stares inside her mug as if searching for answers.

"I was twenty-eight yesterday, and I'm seriously wondering if my life matters."

"Of course it matters. You can knock that thought right out of your mind straight away, young lady! You're a wonderful person."

"Am I though? What have I done that's so wonderful? There's no purpose to my existence. In fact, I'm pretty useless."

"Hey, hey, where is all this coming from?" Dotty leans over and grasps my hand. Her age-spotted skin crinkles as her ever-cold fingers wrap around mine.

Her hand is so cold I automatically place my other hand over it to warm it through. "I need to buy you fingerless gloves, Nana. No matter how high the heating is on your hands are always cold."

"Cold hands, warm heart," she smiles at me.

"I wish I was more like you. You're constantly busy and active, and helping out at church. You always have a kind word and are forever comforting people."

"Firstly, you are more like me than you realize. And secondly, I've been through heartbreak many times. Going through loss alters you in a way you can't understand, until you go through it yourself. It's from my pain that I am able to offer comfort to others."

We are quiet for a moment. I know she will be thinking not only of my granddad but of my mum who died of a brain tumor when I was only eight years old. Dotty repeatedly said the good to come from it was that I had come to live with her, and that I brought life into her heart. My father left my mum when I was only two years old and moved to Australia. During the divorce the lawyers had told mum that he'd met someone and wanted to marry them, and that was why he was pushing for the divorce. I have no memories of him, only two old black and white faded photographs. I don't think I ever missed him until my mum died, then I'd daydreamed that he'd come and fetch me and take me to Australia to live with him. Dotty wrote him but he never replied. So the seeds of worthlessness were sown into my spirit, along with the dagger of rejection that still juts out of my back to this day.

Tears trickle from the corner of my eyes. "I so wanted to be a mum."

"Oh, my little love." Dotty is out of her chair, folding her arms around me as she covers my head with kisses. "There's still time for you to have a family. You just need to find the courage to leave that treacherous cad, and move on with your life. I know you don't think you deserve to be loved, but I tell you, you do. He doesn't cheat on you because you've failed. He cheats because he's weak."

I lean in against her smell of sweetened lavender, the softness of her jumper touching my face. I know there is no comfort in the world that is greater than a hug from a person who loves you. Her warmth flows through me. Her love is like a healing tonic bringing hope into my darkness.

When I've stopped crying, Dotty fishes a handkerchief out of her pocket and dabs at my face. "There is someone in the world that is right for you. You just haven't met him yet, I don't think, but you never know. This person whoever he is will make you feel whole, complete. That great big black hole that drains all your joy," she taps on my chest, "will slowly close, allowing cheerfulness to fill you. I know you can't believe it will happen, but trust me it will, if you let it. Your life is a sum of your choices, just choose wisely."

"Starting with divorce?"

"Yes, I truly believe that should be your first step."

"Then what?"

"Well now then, the world's your oyster as they say. What do you want to do?"

"I've been thinking about my time at university a lot lately."

"You want to go back to studying?"

"No, but I would like to combine my architecture BA with some way of helping people. I have no idea what that might be yet, but it's a dream building inside me."

"Then I will pray it takes root in your soul and leads you to joy."

Chapter 3

AFTER A THOUGHTFUL BUT RELAXING weekend, Monday is here and I need to face the fire. As my car is at home, I've called for a limousine. I don't know why I spot it today, but I've just noticed how much Luke looks like Channing Tatum. We exchange glances through the rear view mirror. His gorgeous blue eyes are questioning, maybe a little concerned.

He's been driving me around for three years, and pretty much all I know about him are three things. His name; he works for Luxury Travel Ltd, and his wife died in a skiing accident four years ago. This he'd shared with me only five months ago, when I'd told him to get himself home to his wife as it was so late. I'd offered sincere condolences, which had managed somehow to feel empty because I'd really not known what to say.

Now I know *four* things, because I've just clocked that his eyes are blue. A slow-burning heat rises up my cheeks. Do I consider myself single already? For goodness' sake, I've not even called the lawyer yet.

I usually let myself out of the car, but today before I've had a chance to pick up my handbag, Luke is opening the door. I lift my chin up as I look at him. His eyes seem to be questioning me, but he obviously can't quite bring himself to say anything. I feel awkward, offer a half smile, whisper 'thanks' and hasten indoors.

I don't know whether to be relieved or cross. For true to his streak of cowardice, Roland has fled. I feel the stress roll off me though, as my shoulders slump while making my way to the study. I've been sitting at the desk for only a minute when Judith comes in carrying a tray.

"Tea?" she asks, putting the tray down on the table.

"Please."

She lifts the tea-cozy off the pot, and pours tea into a delicate teacup, adds a drop of cold milk and passes it to me.

"Are you not having any?" Silly question really, as Judith's only brought one cup in.

"I've just had some. Is there anything I can do for you?"

"Hit my stupid husband on the head and hopefully knock some sense into him?"

"Anything else? Something I won't get arrested for?"

Halfhearted smiles pass between us, as she sits down opposite me.

"I don't suppose he told you where he was going, or when he'd be back?"

"No, sorry. He wasn't in good sorts this morning. He slammed doors all over the house, which is not like him."

"No, it's not. Maybe he can sense that this time I'm really going to leave him?"

"You are?"

"You can't be surprised."

"Well, I know despite everything you actually love him."

"Love, it seems, isn't enough to hold a marriage together. How long have you been married now?"

Judith counts her fingers. "It will be nine years next May."

"Are you still close?"

"Oh yes, very. He's my everything, if you know what I mean. He's such a good dad to Daisy as well. I was certainly blessed the day we were introduced."

"That's nice." I'm overcome with jealousy. Why couldn't I be enough for Roland, why couldn't I have been his everything? Why couldn't I have had a child? "I need to make some phone calls now."

"Yes, of course. I've finished everywhere except the kitchen, so you'll find me there if you need me."

"Thanks Judith."

The emotions going through me are just yuck. I mean really yuck! I feel like a dinghy being bounced by rough seas, battered from all sides and quickly sinking. Before I chicken out, I pick up the phone and call Sebastian.

"Good afternoon, how may I help you?"

"Hello Mary, is Sebastian free please?"

"Oh, hi Charity, hold the line please, I'll just check." She comes back fairly instantly. "He's free, I'll transfer you now."

"Thank you." I'm reminded that it is good practice to be friendly with both your lawyer *and* their secretary.

"Charity, how the devil are you? Sorry I couldn't make your birthday bash on Friday. Did you have a marvelous time?"

"Not really." I can't help laughing.

"Sorry to hear that, what can I do for you today?"

So like a man to not want to know the details. "Have you heard from Roland?"

"Not since he rang to invite me to your party. Is everything alright?"

"I'm divorcing him, and I would really appreciate it if you could handle everything for me. I know you are technically Roland's family lawyer, however, he uses Trevor

& Cornelius for his businesses, so he can go to them for this."

I didn't expect congratulations, or condolences, but the silence really cuts me. I feel judged and extremely uncomfortable. "Of course, if you would prefer to handle things for Roland I'll understand."

"No, no, not at all. It's not that."

"What is it then?"

"Look, I don't want to say anything over the phone, I'd rather come and see you if that's alright with you? Plus, before I see you I need to check some things out. Are you free tomorrow morning, let's say, about ten? I'll call on you at home."

"I wasn't planning on staying here, could you come to my grandmother's house in Holmes Chapel?"

"Yes, of course. I'll put you back to Mary so you can give her the address. Right, I'll see you tomorrow then."

"Sebastian?"

"Yes?"

"Is there something I should be worried about?"

"Look, I don't want to lie to you, but I do need to find out more before I tell you anything. Try not to worry. I'll see you tomorrow."

What on earth was that all about? My mind launches into overdrive, the worst possible scenarios vying for prominence in my too active brain. I start pacing the room. The thought trail that somehow, without my knowledge, Roland has a prenuptial contract hidden away finally demands center stage, although I can't remember signing any contracts. But then I'd been so young and naïve. Would it matter if there was a contract? Did I *really* need to take any money from

23

him? What about my plans to help people? I stop pacing in front of the patio doors and stare into the garden. Everything from the party has been taken away and the lawns are pristine once more.

If I have to walk away with nothing, my life won't be so neat. I have no money of my own, no house, no business, not even a career. Lord, what an idiot I've been. There's movement to the side of the garden and my eyes shift slightly to find Luke talking to Joe, one of the gardeners. I didn't even know they knew each other. What's he still doing here? As if sensing my look, Luke turns his head and studies me. Warmth tingles over my skin. He really is shockingly handsome. He turns back to continue talking to Joe, and I feel the loss of his gaze. What on earth is wrong with me?

Suddenly, an urge to gather anything of mine that is worth anything slams into me. I run over to the safe in the wall behind Roland's desk. Kneeling down I open the fake panel and punch the numbers into the keypad. It doesn't open. I re-try them. It still doesn't open.

"Damn and blast that man!" I should never have given him a warning that I wanted to leave. My most expensive jewelry is in that safe. I pick up my cell and call him; it goes straight to voice mail as if it isn't on. Frustration rips through me and I throw the phone at the wall. It lands with a crunch. I realize straight away that was probably not very clever of me, given that there's a good possibility I'm going to be broke. I pick it up and thankfully it still works.

Judith appears in the doorway. "Everything OK?"

"No, actually, I don't think it is."

We look at each other for a moment. It's hard to know what to say when you think your husband has taken you for a fool and exploited your ignorance. What's that saying again, a fool and his money are soon parted? We'd married as soon as we'd finished university. His parents had tragically died in a plane crash six months earlier, and I had just about held Roland together as he grieved. With only a few weeks left in Cambridge he'd announced he couldn't stand the thought of being without me, so we had married straight away. Only Dotty and two of his friends had attended. Even though we married in St Matthew's Church, near the university, I had worn a simple flowery dress not wanting to spend money on a traditional white dress. It wasn't until he drove us home that I realized he came from extreme wealth. I'd known he had money, of course I did. How many students drive a car, let alone a Ferrari? It hadn't been brand new, but still. But the extent of his father's wealth, obtained from building a hotel chain, only became apparent when he showed me around his estate, my new home.

"I think I'm about to be poor." If I had a different disposition I might have found myself fainting right now. The sudden awakening to how stupid I've been with my life is punching at me: six rounds with Muhammad Ali would be better than the punches I'm throwing at myself. Stupid, stupid, stupid girl! I've wasted my life. I've done nothing with my architecture qualifications, and who would want me now? How am I going to get a job when all I can write on my CV is lady of leisure, throws excellent dinner parties, can swim for hours, oh and has very good dress sense!

Judith walks over and places a hand on my arm. "I'm sure Mr. Byron will look after you."

"Maybe, but something tells me it's not going to be plain sailing. Will you help me pack please, Judith? I'd planned on taking just a few things, but I think it might be best if I take everything I consider to be mine."

Three hours later, I'm standing on the drive surrounded by a pile of suitcases and boxes. I had taken more clothes than I would need with the thought I might be able to sell the ball gowns. Thankfully, my personal jewelry box is still full. I wish now that I preferred big pieces of jewelry, liking small dainty pieces meant the price of them was far less than what Roland would happily have spent on me. I keep muttering 'que sera sera', and I'm dying to burst into my best Doris Day impression!

There are seven cars in the garage. I've asked Joe if he will fetch the Range Rover for me. I figure it will take most of the stuff I've packed, plus it's the most sensible car in the garage. It's also one of two cars that are actually registered in my name. Many hands make light work and soon the three of us have filled the car to capacity, I'll just be able to see out through the mirrors.

"Is there anything else?" asks Joe as he closes the boot.

"Nothing that I can say is mine," I answer with a weary smile.

Joe hovers and I get the distinct impression he would like to hug me, I take a quick step towards the car. I don't think I can handle sympathy right now.

"I'll come back in a few days, make sure everything is OK. Just call me if you need me. You have my grandmother's phone number don't you?"

Judith nods. She's also trying to hold back tears.

Too much pain! I dive into the Rover, turn, give a feeble wave, and then I'm off down the driveway. I'll come back soon and make sure everyone is alright, but first I need to sort my head out and figure out what I want to do with the rest of my life. That's after the harbinger of bad news arrives tomorrow, and tells me exactly what's going on.

Chapter 4

I'D BEEN UP SINCE FIVE. After going for a jog in the damp, cold darkness, I'd returned for a long shower and tons of coffee. Normally a run would sooth me, but today my nerves are like electric shocks, zinging me to death! The last half an hour has been spent pacing the kitchen, and I was glad when Dotty decided she just *had* to have some fresh cakes to offer Sebastian when he arrives. I guess she really just needs some peace for a little while. No doubt she will be praying for me too, which actually even as a non-believer I feel quite comforted by.

It's nearly quarter past ten when both Sebastian and Dotty approach the front door at the same time. I hear Dotty going on about how mild this December is as they approach the kitchen.

"Morning," Sebastian's smile is wide and warm. He doesn't look like a person about to deliver dire news.

"Hi. Would you like to go into the living room, or is here suitable?" I gesture towards the kitchen table.

"Wherever is most comfortable for you."

"Let's stay here then." I try to smile at him, but I can feel the awfulness of it, and sit down quickly.

"Tea or coffee anyone?" asks Dotty.

We both confirm we'd like a cup of coffee. As the filter's been ready since ten all she has to do is fill two cups, which she brings over with a plate full of different fancies. "I have some things to do, so I will leave you to it."

"Thanks Nana." She pats my shoulder before leaving, her way of saying 'it will be alright, and I'm here for you.' My throat tightens, and I have to force myself to take a breath and focus. "So, you have some news for me?" I didn't know how else to begin, and I couldn't beat about the bush, I really needed to hear the bad news sooner rather than later.

"Well, as you probably gathered from our phone call, there are certain things going on that I believe you are unaware of." He stifles a little cough.

Oh, for crying out loud, please tell me. "What things?"

Sebastian takes a drink of coffee, delaying tactics I guess as he tries to find the right words to tell me. "It came to my attention two years ago, that Roland is gambling, quite heavily so."

"What?" This wasn't what I was expecting. Why is he telling me this?

"He asked me to witness a promissory note." Sebastian's leaning forward, talking slowly as if to a child. I feel as if a huge sledge-hammer is slowly swinging towards my head. "He was in debt to Roxy's Casino to the tune of two and a half million. They refused him any more credit until he cleared it. As he didn't have that amount in cash, he asked me to set up a promissory note stating he would pay it as soon as he sold the yacht."

"He's sold the Blue Byron!" My heart is hammering. That was his dad's treasured possession. I can't believe Roland has sold it.

"He did. I'm afraid that's not all."

I want to get up and scream. What's going on? Roland is a coke and sex addict. When did he start big-time gambling? "Tell me." My hands are shaking as I place them on my lap.

"He repeated the request just six months ago, for a similar amount. I'm afraid he sold the Spanish villa."

I feel sick. My head is swimming. Is Sebastian going to tell me we're broke?

"Are you OK, Charity?"

I nod.

"He has been coming to me for the last six months instructing me to sell various antiques and paintings from around the house."

"I'm a fool. I asked him what was happening with the paintings that were getting replaced by modern pieces. He told me he wanted a more modern feel and was slowing replacing the old stuff with new." A thought strikes me. "Do we still own the house? What about the hotels? Are they safe?"

"As far as I am aware both the house and the hotel chain haven't been touched yet. But I must be honest; he might have had Trevor & Cornelius deal with it. After we spoke yesterday, I had a meeting with a friend of mine who works there. He said he hadn't heard of the hotels being sold and he was sure he would have heard if they had been. So I think we can safely assume the house and business are still intact."

"And there's no prenuptial contract?"

"What? Oh, sorry. I didn't think yesterday after my cryptic conversation that you would think that. No, there is no contract. You have been married for seven years so you will receive a settlement. Obviously, the business and house are Roland's inheritance, so I think you would have quite a battle on your hands if you wanted fifty per cent."

30

"Goodness, no. I'd never dream of asking for half. I am, however, very grateful to know that I will receive something."

"Right then, I'll get the paperwork started and contact Roland to see what sort of offer he is happy to make, and then we'll go from there."

"I hope you have better luck than me trying to get hold of him. I've been calling his cell since yesterday morning with no response." Lightness is dancing inside me. It wasn't total bad news after all, how blooming marvelous! I knew the last time the business had been evaluated it had been valued at thirty million, and the house was about two million, so if Roland was happy to give it, I would be happy with half a million, and if he felt generous and wanted to give me one million that would be even better. I figure that would be enough for me to start a charitable business. What type of charity I have no idea yet, but I plan to do loads of research and see where I can help out best. If I can do something within the housing sector, I might even be able to put my masters to use.

I must have zoned out because I realize Sebastian has been talking to me. "Sorry what did you say?"

"I said I should get going. The sooner I can contact Roland the quicker we can get this ball rolling."

"Oh, yes of course. Thanks so much for driving out to me. I really appreciate it."

We stand and walk to the door. Dotty appears to say goodbye. As we watch him walk down the drive to his car, I slip my hand in Nana's.

She gives my hand a quick squeeze. "Everything going to be alright?"

I turn and give her a big hug. "Yes Nana, I think everything's going to be fine."

The phone in the hallway starts ringing.

"I wonder who that can be?" says Dotty getting up out of the armchair. It's one of those little things that amuse me, that she refuses to get the phone moved into the living room, 'got to keep moving,' she says, 'go stiff as a board otherwise.' I listen to her speaking and realize that the call is for me. As I get up to go into the hallway, she calls out.

"Charity, it's Judith for you."

"Thanks," I say taking the phone from her. "Hi Judith, is everything OK?"

"Mrs. Bryon, there are gentlemen here to see you. I'm afraid they won't leave until they've spoken with you."

"Really? Who?"

"He's say his name is Mr. Green and that he works for the Hollingworth jewelers."

"Hollingworth, the jewelers?"

"I believe so."

"Please put him on the phone." My stomach is whooshing back and forth like the tide, so much so that I'm tottering on the verge of being mighty sea sick.

"Good afternoon Mrs. Bryon." The voice is deep and very business-like.

"Good afternoon, tell me how can I help you?"

"We have come to collect the Blue Nile necklace, which was lent to your husband for your birthday party, I believe."

"Lent?"

"Yes, it was on loan to heighten its publicity. Mr. Byron was due to return it to the office yesterday, unfortunately he never appeared. Do you have the necklace, Mrs. Bryon?"

Invisible hands are clasped around my throat, threatening to strangle me. "No," I whisper.

"Do you know where it might be?"

"I assume it's in the safe in the study."

"Would you mind coming back to the house please and opening the safe to check? We really would prefer not to involve the police at this stage."

Police! I sit down with a bump on the stool next to the telephone table. "It will take me an hour to get ready and come home. Is it possible for you to come back tomorrow morning please?"

"I'm afraid we can't do that madam. If we are unable to retrieve the necklace today, we will go straight to the police. An hour is fine. We will wait here for you."

"Can you put me back on the phone with my housekeeper, please?"

"Of course. We shall see you later."

"Mrs. Byron?"

"Hi Judith, can you please show them into the drawing room and offer them refreshments?"

"Yes of course. Is there anything else I can do?"

"No, that's fine. I'll see you soon."

"You're as white as a ghost," says Dotty after I've put the phone down.

"Roland didn't buy me that necklace, he only borrowed it."

"Well that's alright, isn't it dear? You don't like it anyway."

33

"I don't mind giving it back. The problem is Roland has changed the code on the safe, and I don't know how to get in to get it for them. If I can't give it to them today, they're going to the police."

"Well we'd best find a way to get into the safe then," said Dotty, "I'll get the yellow pages and we'll start looking for a locksmith."

"I've got my iPad, Nana. I'll look on the internet."

It takes half an hour and ten phone calls before I finally talk to someone who can open a Chubb Trident safe for me within the hour. I confirm the address and agree to meet him at the house as soon as possible.

"Would you like me to come with you, dear?" asks Dotty as I'm putting on my coat.

"No, it's fine. Judith will be there. I'll be OK."

"Ring me when it is sorted."

I give her a kiss on the cheek. "Will do."

I'm shaking like a leaf as I drive. I wish I'd had time to call Luke, I don't think I should be driving. The nerves are at an atomic level of stress for I have a horrid suspicion the necklace won't be there, and I have no idea what I can do if it's not. I try Roland's cell, yet again. It goes straight to voice mail. Where the heck is he? I could throttle him right now.

As it turns out the locksmith has arrived before me. Stuffing my hands in my pockets to hide their shaking, I hasten inside. Judith rushes to meet me in the hallway. Her face is white and I'm ashamed to have her worry. I force a smile.

"It'll be OK, Judith. Can you show them into the study please?"

She nods and heads into the drawing room as I make my way into the study.

Judith appears with three men, two of whom are smartly dressed in suits, Hollingworth's men then.

"Please come in," I say, trying to keep my voice steady.

I look at the third man who is carrying a metal case. "Thank you for coming on such short notice, the safe is over here." I point to the wall panel which is open, displaying the safe.

"You're welcome," he answers coming over. "This happens all the time, you'd be surprised. Shall we get straight to it?"

"Yes please," I answer, slowly putting my hands behind my back and crossing my fingers, something I've not done since I was thirteen.

I'm totally shocked when he opens it in less than a minute. So much for security! I'm also shocked when he tells me the charge for an immediate call out is two hundred and fifty! After I've handed him a check, Judith escorts him to the door, leaving me with the men most eager to retrieve a very expensive diamond necklace.

My knees are shaking as I kneel on the floor. Oh, God, if you are real, please let the necklace be here. There are several jewelry boxes in the safe, and tons of paperwork, and to my utmost relief so is the purple velvet case that the necklace came in. I lift it out and with trembling fingers lift the lid. A whoosh of air escapes my lungs as I happily smile up at the men after seeing the necklace is there.

The taller gentleman takes the box from me and puts it on the table. He lifts a loupe eye piece out of his pocket and starts inspecting the necklace. I don't realize I'm holding my breath until he puts it away and turns to me and nods.

"Thank you for your assistance Mrs. Byron, it is much appreciated."

"You're most welcome." I feel lightheaded and sit down behind the desk. "Would you mind showing yourselves out?" My lips are trembling and I'm sure it's easy to see I'm a mess.

"Good afternoon." With no haste the two men stroll out of the study into the hallway. I can hear Judith talking to them. She must have been waiting for them. Good old Judith. As soon as the front door closes, she rushes into the study.

"Is everything OK?"

It isn't, but what do I reply? "Have you heard from Roland at all?"

"Not a dickybird."

"I met with Sebastian today. He's going to represent me."

"Oh, that's good. Fine gentleman he is. Do you want me to put all this back in the safe for you?"

I look at the pile. "While I am here I might as well go through things, see what other secrets Roland may be keeping. You can help me put it all on the table please."

It only takes a moment and the contents of the safe are spread across the desk.

"This one's got your name on it," says Judith handing me an envelope. I recognize Roland's scrawl straight away.

"Can this day get any worse?" I ask. Judith doesn't answer. Where instant, clear knowledge comes from I have no idea. All I can say is that I suddenly *know* what's in the envelope. "Judith, would you mind very much popping the kettle on please?"

"Yes of course. Would you like some green tea?"

"Just normal tea, please."

I wait until she's left before picking up the letter opener and slicing the envelope open. I pull out three sheets of writing paper.

> *My love,*
>
> *Please forgive me. That is all I ask of you. It sounds simple, and yet I know I ask for something I do not deserve. If you are reading this letter then by now you will know that I have taken the coward's way out. I cannot face you learning the truth of all my lies and secrets, which will surely come to light when the solicitors start the divorce proceedings. To watch love fade in your eyes is more than I can bear.*
>
> *I am sorry that I couldn't live up to your expectations, that I couldn't remain that knight in shining armor that you dreamed of when you were young.*
>
> *Thank you for looking after me when my parents died, I truly believe that without you I would probably have over-dosed during those days. Your love kept me away from cocaine when I felt bemused and alone.*

What you will find out later, is that I have AIDS. I have had it for two years now, which is why my love I have not come to your room for two years. I know you think it is the other women that keep me away, but in truth I couldn't tell you so I kept letting you find out about other women to put you off me. I expected you to leave me a long time ago. I am not sure why you stayed, though I confess I longed to believe it was because you never stopped loving me.

What a mess I've made of my life.

Don't waste yours, sweet Charity. Please take whatever money is left and do something amazing with your life. I leave everything I have to you. Sebastian has a copy of my will.

Forgive me if you can,
Your idiot of a husband....
Roland x

Tears have been flowing the whole time I read, but now I've finished reading the tears are turning into sobs. I never understood those people who wailed at the death of their loved ones, but I find my body has decided *I* am one of those people. Wailing reaches into the depths of my being and then surges upwards and outwards with fog-horn loudness. I can hardly breathe as scream after scream rips from my throat. How could he take his own life? I've done research on cocaine when I first realized Roland's habit was out of control. I know that drugs can lead to serious depression, but I had no idea how low he must have been. Why didn't I see? How could he leave me? *Roland!*

I don't notice Judith rush into the study, I only become aware of her presence when she wraps her arms around me and sobs with me. I cling onto her as if my life depends on it. My tears soak her shoulder. My ears are ringing. The room is spinning…

Chapter 5

I'VE BEEN WALKING FOR FOUR HOURS. My feet are beginning to protest, but gosh, my head is clear. I can see the Methodist Church up ahead, so I'm nearly back at Dotty's. I know she will have been worried about me, but I needed to grab a rare sunny day to stretch my legs. And dissect the last two months.

After scanning a copy of Roland's letter over to Sebastian, he had instantly contacted the police for me. It had taken the police just two days to find Roland's body. He'd overdosed in a flat in Wilmslow, which belongs to one of his friends who is currently living in London. A coroner had been appointed and cause of death report compiled. Identifying his body had been so shocking I'd been unable to get out of bed for two days. I slept a lot of the shock and stress away. The press had been dreadful and to keep them away from Dotty I'd returned to live in the house for a short time.

Besides the funeral and dealing with thousands of condolences, I'd had numerous meetings with Trevor & Cornelius. The news wasn't so good, but I'd kind of been expecting it. More than half the hotels had been sold one by one over the last few years. Only three remained, the value of which they confirmed should be in the region of three to four million. Byron's wasn't the empire it used to be, but between the hotels and the house it looked like my charitable-venture would happen after all. Everything had gone up for sale immediately. The house had sold within a week, which totally shocked me. But the hotels were still up for sale, with apparently not much interest. Still, it's early days yet.

I'd sold, or given to charity, nearly everything in the house, and arranged for decorators to blast through leaving everything tip-top for the new owners. For the time being I'm staying with Dotty, but I have my eyes open, looking for a cottage style house around Wilmslow. With that in mind, I continue to pay Judith who is happy to stay with me. The gardeners I had to let go, but I'd given them generous payoffs and glowing references.

It was the end of an era. The 'do nothing but look glamorous' part of my life was over. From now on I'm going to do something meaningful. I would really like to leave something behind. If I could take Roland's remaining inheritance and turn it into something that helped people, then in a way, his legacy would live on.

As I walk up the drive, the front door flies open. Nana, bless her, has her stern face on. "Where have you been? I've been worried sick."

"Sorry. I just lost track of time. I feel calm now though, if that helps you feel less cross with me at all?"

Dotty tuts. "You had a visitor," she says shutting the door behind me and closing off the biting February wind.

"I did? Who was it?"

"A very nice young man, called Luke."

I freeze, mid coat removing, and stare at her. "What did he want?"

"Get that coat and boots off too, and let's go into the kitchen." She heads off without waiting for me, and now as quickly as possible I'm hanging up my coat, pulling off my boots, and chasing after her.

"Well?" I ask, impatience raising my blood pressure.

"He just wanted to check on you, see how you're doing. He waited an hour for you, but in the end he said he needed to get to work."

I sink into the chair, gazing at the table-top. I'm scrambling around my brain trying to ascertain how I feel. I'm touched he thought to see how I'm doing. I'm also sad I wasn't here to see him. Now why is that? I hadn't thought about him since finding Roland's letter, but now I find myself soaked in little memories. The color of his eyes. The way he smiles. His muscular body. His deep, smooth voice that sends goose bumps up and down my arms. I wish I'd been home.

"Did he leave a message?"

Dotty joins me at the table, pushing a mug towards me. "Get your hands around that hot cocoa, it will warm you up."

I pull the drink towards me, wrapping both hands around the steaming mug. Dotty puts her hand in her apron pocket, pulls out a card and hands it to me. At first, I'm disappointed as I can see it's a Luxury Travel business card. But when I turn it over I can't help smiling. He's written, *Sorry I missed you. Call if you ever need a friend.* Then he'd written down his cell number. I'm not looking for a new relationship, but knowing Luke is offering friendship warms my soul. I tuck the card in my jeans pocket.

"He seems very nice." She's scrutinizing my face, and I can't help chuckling.

42

"He is indeed. He's also just a *friend*."

"Well, you can never have too many friends... and of course if they're good-looking, that's just a bonus. He reminds me of that actor in Magic Mike."

"You never saw that film... did you?"

"Ha, ha, ha, you should see your face. Yes, we watched it on one of our ladies nights a while back. I just covered my eyes in the bits that were too raunchy."

"You learn something new every day! What else have you watched?"

"Movie night happens once a month, so I've seen quite a lot of films actually. What I love more than the films though is the chat afterwards where we break down the movie into what was good or bad. We have some quite heated conversations."

"I bet you do."

After a moment's silence, Dotty takes a deep breath before asking. "What happens next?"

"I'll probably send him a text saying thank you for calling."

"That's not what I mean. What are you going to do with your life?"

"I'd like to live in Wilmslow. Judith lives in Lacey Green, so it will be really quick for her to get to work. I've seen some quaint places around The Carrs Park. After I've settled in I'd like to find a charitable company who will take me on as a volunteer, so I can learn how things work. Maybe for two years, while I figure out what kind of venture I want to start."

"Why the two-year delay?"

"I guess I'm not confident enough in my own abilities to just jump into it."

"My sweet girl, you have to believe in yourself. Dig deep and find your courage. Fear is the joy thief. You have been in hiding for years now. Afraid to poke your head out in case something bad happens. Now don't look at me like that, I know you well." She flaps her hand at me. "All so beautiful and elegant, so lady-like and perfect. Yet inside you're a bubbling mess who teeters on the edge of depression, that ugly soul crusher. In fear that something bad might happen you don't move forward with your life. I'm telling you my girl… that is no way to live."

I can't reply. A massive lump has lodged in my throat.

"I understand that your father's rejection hit you hard, but you can't define yourself by someone else's mistakes. Live your own life, make your own mistakes."

"I think having no parents is what cemented mine and Roland's relationship. Our sorrow glued us together. I think if his parents hadn't been in an accident we would never have married."

"Ifs and buts pull you down. Forget them. Your life is what it is; you have forever to mold yourself into whatever type of person you want to be. Who do you want to be, Charity? And I don't mean what you want to do, I mean *who* do you want to *be*."

There's a warm glow massaging my skin and filling my heart. "I want to be bold, independent, passionate and energetic. I want to help people. I want to build something."

"That's my girl. Hopefully, you won't want to do it all on your own though. Don't confuse independent with being single. There is a man out there who will tie you down with

44

arms of love and yet at the same time, set you free to be you."

"I'm not sure that's possible."

"I am. Your grandfather, God bless his soul, was such a man. I pray that you will find your man, just like I did."

Later that night, all enthused from Nana's positive pep talk, I text Luke. Just to say thanks for calling. His answer is instant.

I'm glad you're OK. It would be nice if we could meet up sometime, when you're feeling up to it. Luke x

Chapter 6

I'M NOT SURE HOW IT HAPPENED, but texting Luke had turned into a full time thing. The next morning he'd sent a text just saying good morning, I'd replied, and here we are three days later meeting up for a walk in the grounds of Tatton Park.

Both early risers, Luke had picked me up at 9.30 am and driven us to the car park inside Tatton grounds. It had felt strange at first, getting into his Ford Mondeo and sitting in the front. Whether he felt awkward or not, I'll never know because he chatted away about all sorts until I finally relaxed.

"You going to be warm enough?" Luke asks.

I'm well wrapped up, in woolly hat and matching scarf and thick fur-lined mittens, warm coat and flower-power walking boots. Luke gives the boots a smirk.

"They are the most comfortable and water-proof footwear I have," I snip.

"They'll need to be," answers Luke nodding towards the landscape before us.

Mist rolls across a frost-bitten land. The sun is only just beginning to break through the morning's clouds. Parts of the ground are still white; other parts where the rays have broken through are a mixture of brown and green. Sheep move in the distance, dots of life before a background of eerie woods. The world is still and blissfully quiet, if somewhat wet.

"Ready?"

I've got my scarf pulled over my mouth and nose, so I nod. My eyes are sparkling with life though. I pull my gaze from his full lips up to his eyes, to find they're smiling at me. Twinkling with life and fun. We head off down a path that will take us around the mansion and down to Tatton Mere. We plan to walk around the lake and then back up to the Tea Rooms for a cup of coffee, and hopefully some scones and cream, a terrible breakfast I know but I'm looking forward to a change from toast.

We walk without the need to talk. Both of us are soaking in the natural beauty of the frost-sprinkled park. We've been walking for about half-an-hour, when Luke suddenly grabs my arm, while pointing with his other hand. Off in the distance stands a lone stag. A majestic deer, standing still but poised for running, his head lifted, impressive antlers resting on his head like a crown. Does he see us? After a short moment, he drops his head and grazes. Into the mist-soaked clearing a herd of female deer delicately pick their way.

"Wow, so many doe for just one stag, talk about stud!"

"Lucky guy, aye," Luke says leaning in close.

"Oh, I don't know. Could you imagine having eight wives hanging onto your coat tails all day long, every day?"

Luke laughs. "Ah, well if you put it like that. Mind you though... I wouldn't mind having at least one." He looks straight into my eyes, and I freeze like a rabbit in the headlights. My heart's thumping irregularly and heat rises up from my neck. Before I can think of any witty repartee, Luke has turned around.

"Come on, or we'll never get this walk done," he says, obviously totally unaware of my near panic attack. For the next hour we talk about family. I'm surprised at the ease with which I pour out what happened to my parents, as I've shared this with hardly anyone before.

"That's tough," he answers after I finish telling him about my dad.

"What are your parents like?" I ask, trying to deflect the 'I'm sorry' that I knew would follow.

"Both mum and dad are alive and well, I'm blessed to say. They're both retired now. Mum used to work as a doctor's receptionist and dad drove lorries for a living. They live in Stockport, so not far away. I normally spend Sundays with them. Mum says I wouldn't go to church unless I picked them up, and dad says I wouldn't come at all if mum didn't make such great Sunday roasts!" Luke chortles away to himself. I realize it is the first time I've heard him laugh. Gosh, but it's a wonderful sound.

Something occurs to me. If they've retired they must be over sixty-five, and if that's the case how old is Luke? "Did they have you late in life?" Blimey but that sounds rude, still there's no taking it back now.

Luke roars. When he calms down, he asks. "Why do I look young?"

I'm unsure of myself now. I thought he looked around thirty. I opt for safe and just shrug.

"I was thirty-eight November just gone."

"Oh!" I can't help having such an expressive face. It's practically impossible to hide how I'm feeling.

"What? Am I too old for you?" He's messing with me, I can tell by the crow lines that crinkle around his eyes as he smiles at me. I gently knock his arm.

"Come on old man, I've got a yearning for coffee and cake."

With soft smiling eyes, Luke nods, and we make our way back along the path beside the lake.

"How was your walk?" asks Dotty.

"Actually, it was lovely."

Nana smiles, her rosy cheeks set off her speckled cornflower-blue eyes. It seems to me that no matter how wrinkled and age-spot covered her face becomes, her eyes are just as vibrant today as they were when I was a child.

"That's good, and do you plan on meeting again soon?"

"It's way too early for me to start dating, Nana."

"Is it? Why's that?"

This indignant reaction whooshes through me making me nauseous. I feel my face become ugly – as Nana would describe it, with a scrunched up nose and an upside down smile. "I've only just buried Roland!"

"Less of that uppityness, young lady! You might have only just buried his body, but your marriage had been dead for years."

I can't stop the tears that flood my eyes and spill down my cheeks. "I know, but I did love him and he's only just gone."

Dotty comes over to sit on the sofa with me. Wrapping her arms around me she strokes my hair. "You have been unhappy for years. It is time to let go."

"I will. I just think it's going to take me some time."

Dotty pushes back to look at me. She plants a hand on each of my shoulders. I pull a hanky out of my pocket and give my nose a quick blow.

"There isn't time to mess around with trying to sort out your feelings and emotions. That navel-gazing is destroying your joy. Be brave. Be courageous. Look up instead of down. If there is chance of happiness today you must grab it, because I can tell you happiness in tomorrow is not guaranteed."

"I think that's easier said than done."

Nana tuts, taking her hands down onto her lap. Her chin is wobbling.

"Nana, what's wrong?" It's my turn to lean forward and wrap my hands around hers. She's trembling. "Nana! You're worrying me, what's wrong? You're not ill are you?" Panic. Pure acid-filled adrenalin surges through me and I feel faint. I can't lose her as well.

"While you were out, I popped next door to have a cuppa with Cathy."

"Are Cathy and Mike OK?"

She nods. "When I was there, their daughter Shirley came over. She was in a right tither. She showed us a video she had on her phone." Dotty's frail body crumbles, her shoulders shaking as she sobs.

"What is it?" I can't keep the fright out of my voice.

"Sorry love, sorry."

I pass her a few tissues and she blows her nose with a loud honk.

"What was on the phone?"

"A Chinese lady. She's a nurse and had a white mask over her face. She took her cell around the hospital where she works in Wuhan. Oh love, it was terrible. The hospital was packed. She showed dead people covered in cloths.

Women were howling in the background. It was just dreadful, dreadful."

"Why would Shirley show you that?" Anger's quickly rising.

"The nurse was warning the world about what's happening over there. She said it's a virus called Coronavirus and that one person can infect fourteen others in one day. Shirley said after she watched it she searched the internet for other references. Apparently, it's just been named COVID-19 and it's been known about since December. World leaders have been informed about it, but no one is doing anything. The nurse said that there are ninety thousand people affected in Wuhan alone."

"I'm sure that's not right. It's probably fake news."

"All the reports on-line say it's going to kill thousands of people in every country in the world."

"Nana, you know there are doomsday people who love to make these claims, they never amount to anything. Thousands of people die in England each year from flu and nobody bats an eyelid, this virus is probably just another strain of the flu, you'll see, it will be fine."

Dotty straightens up. Her chin has gone into the square-set that usually means she's brooking no nonsense. "And what if it isn't? Have you ever thought that you actually don't know what tomorrow is going to bring? What if this virus strikes us like none before it? What if millions around the world die from it?" She leans forward and squints at me. "What if your young man Luke catches it? What then? You need to live for today. Forget yesterday, don't fear tomorrow, just be alive in this moment."

Against the inner shrinking I experience about getting emotionally involved with anyone, the truth of her words ring bells inside my head. This is obviously fake news, still I find myself pausing. We don't know what's around the corner. If anything Roland has shown me that.

Chapter 7

IT'S A BIT OF A MYSTERY TO ME how she's managed it, but somehow the crafty old thing has me sitting in church with her. I've tucked myself into the corner of the pew, fixing Nana as my shield against the onslaught of her friends who want to be introduced.

"Sorry about that," whispers Dotty as everyone finally leaves to take their seats.

"I feel like a fish in a tank," I hiss back as quietly as possible. I don't do strangers very well. I never know what to say to them. I invariably feel stupid and uninteresting, it must roll off me too for it isn't long before people normally turn around, obviously bored or disappointed.

"Well, with all that bling, I guess people could mistake you for a goldfish easily enough."

"Nana!" Now I'm drowning in self-doubt. I haven't put on much jewelry. I glance down at my hands. A huge diamond sits next to my wedding ring, and on the other hand I'm wearing my favorite ring which I love, a ruby surrounded by small diamonds. A bit much for church maybe? Not sure why though.

"Your rings are fine. It's your lobe-stretchers I take umbrage with."

My hand automatically goes to the set of gold rings hanging from my right ear. "What's wrong with them?" The question is high-pitched as self-defense kicks in fast.

"They're practically touching your knickers."

I burst out laughing. "They don't even touch my shoulders, Nana."

She winks at me, and I realize she'd just been winding me up. I exhale a long, slow sigh as I reach out and grab her hand. She always knows how to bring me out of myself.

The last time I came to church, besides my marriage, was just before I left to go to university. I have mixed sentiments. I have fond memories of Sunday school and playing with the other kids, I especially used to love the nativity plays. Dotty was regularly doing something to help around the church and the environment had become a sort of second home, more importantly, it had definitely been a second, much-needed family. Though I had enjoyed the social involvements, from the moment mum had died I'd decided God couldn't possibly be real. Since leaving to go to university, I'd also grown averse to the possibility of some white-bearded man sitting in the sky frowning down on all that I do. I especially can't stand the idea that someone can listen in on all my thoughts. They're private, and mine. Gosh, if people knew my thoughts… ugh, I just shudder at the prospect.

The service proceeds in a manner which I remember well. I love the hymns, the music and words have a way of reaching deep inside me. I will not cry. I will *not* cry. Darn, I pull a hankie out of my cuff and dab at the corner of my eyes, hoping Dotty won't notice. Eyes in the back of her head is how I've thought of her many times, and even though she doesn't stop singing or turn her head, she reaches out and takes my hand. No stopping the tears now as they stream down my face. Oh Lord, if you are real, then I'm really sorry for the mess I've made of my life.

Near the end of the service the minister announces a guest speaker, a woman called Megan Munroe who has come to talk about the power of prayer. A small, slim, brunette steps up to the front. She immediately catches my interest. She looks fragile yet powerful at the same time. Her countenance oozes quiet confidence, and I find myself sitting up straight. As she begins to talk, goose-bumps prickle my arms and back. I find myself holding my breath. My heart rate quickens. From nowhere, and with no explanation, excitement builds in my spirit. I'm finding it hard to digest what she's saying, something about Ephesians and the full armor of God. I'm zoning in and out. My skin is prickling, my temperature rising. What's happening to me?

Everything becomes absolutely still. The church is empty. There is no sound. No breath. Just stillness. Into this anointed moment in time, Megan's voice suddenly becomes crystal clear, as if she's talking directly to me.

"We are encouraged in all that we do by the fruits of our labor. God has clearly given us a new mission on top of the ones we already have. We are looking for a place to take children from both orphanages and poor homes on holiday to Wales. We are excited! I am convinced the Lord has told us that he will use this place to bless these children. That He will touch their hearts and give them joy. So we are reaching out to as many people as possible. We are looking for volunteers and also for funding. If you would like to be a part of this, then we would love to talk with you at the end of the service."

A red-hot poker sensation jabs me in the butt causing me to fly out of my seat. All eyes, in a church that is once more packed with people, turn in my direction. My face is burning in embarrassment. I clutch the back of the pew in front of me to steady my feet. Not content with shifting me to my feet the poker somehow jolts my throat.

"I would very much like to be a part of your project," I declare. No idea why I said that! Me, speak out in public, never!

The charismatic brunette smiles at me. Tension slides off my body like huge boulders. I feel light and full of joy. I smile back.

"That's wonderful. Please stay after the service so we can have a chat." Megan finishes her talk, but I've gone back to not being able to hear what she's saying. I'm cocooned in a bubble of joy that I just don't want to burst. Is this it? Is this how I can use Roland's money to build something in his name? What a worthy cause.

I'm glad when the service is finished. I need to know more of their plans and ideas. Why Wales? Accommodation for how many? Who will run it? Agh! I've so much running through my head. I follow Dotty into the church hall, where people have been asked to stay and have drinks.

"Cup of tea, dear?"

I shake my head. "No thanks, Nana. You go though."

She pats my hand and turns to instantly start talking to some of her cronies as they line-up for the refreshment hatch.

"Hello."

I turn around to find a sexy looking guy with black hair and brilliant blue eyes smiling at me. "Hi," I reply.

He holds out his right hand. "I'm Jack, Megan's husband."

"Oh, hello. I'm Charity." I don't know whether to be disappointed or relieved that he's married. What is happening to me these days? He's certainly got come-to-bed eyes. Geez!! And that's why *no one* should be able to hear my thoughts!

"Shall we take a seat and have a chat?" Jack indicates a table close by.

I look around. Does this mean Megan won't be talking to me? I'm disappointed. Am I not worthy of the actual guest speaker? "Yes, sure thing," I answer, heading straight for the nearest table.

"Would you like a drink before we begin?"

"No thank you. I do have a lot of questions."

"Of course. Why don't I tell you a little about the project first, and then you can ask away?"

I 'umm' and nod.

Jack explains how they first started working with teenagers and younger children doing various youth projects, and helping out at youth centers. He explained about the poverty they'd witnessed and also the sadness which so many children live with, and how they had prayed asking God for a way to bring some joy into their lives.

"It was only two weeks ago that one of our friends, a neighbor in fact called Danielle, told us of a wonderful holiday she'd had in a place called Beddgelert in Wales. While she was there she'd seen this set of houses called Gelert Cottages, and noticed that they were up for sale. The location is stunning and just perfect for what we believe God has planned. The property value is 1.2 million, but we will need three times that much to convert it and then maintain it. Do you think this would be something you'd like to volunteer with?"

"Yes!" There is no hesitation. I know deep inside that even without further information, this is something I have to do. Purpose is flooding my veins. Happiness making me dizzy.

"That's wonderful. We have a meeting at our house this week for anyone interested in helping. If you could attend, then you will find out a lot more out about both us and the project."

"I'd love to come. Just say when and let me have the address."

Jack pulls a small notepad out of his pocket and scribbles down their address and phone number before handing it to me.

"We're meeting on Wednesday at 7 pm. We'll be doing a buffet, so don't worry if you haven't eaten."

"That's lovely thank you. I look forward to it."

"Can I ask… are you looking at volunteering full or part-time?"

"I'm not sure yet. I have a notion it will be full time though."

Suddenly, I can't wait to get home. I want to phone Luke and tell him all about it. A thought occurs to me. "Would it be alright if I bring along a friend on Wednesday?"

"Absolutely, the more the merrier." Jack's blue eyes twinkle and I can't help smiling. It sure is a good job he's married.

"See you then," I say standing up.

He stands up and we shake hands.

I spot Dotty across the room talking to a group of ladies. I wait for her to catch my eyes, and then I point at the door to let her know I'm going home. She smiles lifting her cup to show she's still drinking and will stay a bit. I smile softly as I leave. It's not a cup of tea that keeps Nana here; it's the love of true friends.

"Hi." I wonder if Luke can hear me smiling.

"Hi Charity, how's your day going?"

His voice is mellow and I get this image of melted butter on toast, so yummy. "Good so far, I've just been to church actually."

"And you didn't run out during the sermon?"

I'm all warm and cozy, because this man has only been on one walk and coffee date with me, but already seems to know me. "No, in fact quite the opposite, I stayed after it was finished to talk to the guest speaker." I launch, with much enthusiasm, into details of the morning and the youth project.

"Wow, that sounds exciting."

"I'm glad you said that."

"How come?"

"Well I was hoping you might be able to come to the meeting at seven on Wednesday?"

"I'd love to. I'm supposed to be working, but Keith owes me a swap, so I'll give him a call."

"I don't want to put you out, don't worry if you can't come."

"You're not putting me out. In fact, I'm quite excited."

"You are?"

"Yes. This is the first time you've asked me out."

"It's not a date or anything."

Luke bellows down the phone. "Well thank goodness for that, I'd hate to be under that much pressure."

I think he's taking the mickey out of me, but I can't help my insecurity from responding before I have time to stop it. "Are you saying I'm hard work?"

His laughing stops instantly. "No Charity, I'm not saying that at all."

Someone in the background calls, 'dinner's ready Luke.'

"Sounds like your roast is being served, I'll leave you to it."

"I'll pick you up on Wednesday. Where do they live?"

"Blackshaw Moor, do you know it?"

"Yes. It borders the Peak District. It's not too far away from Buxton. I'll pick you up at 6.15 pm if that's OK?"

"Perfect, see you then."

I go into the kitchen to check on the pot-roast we put in the oven before going to church. The smell in the kitchen is wonderful. I hadn't realized that I missed cooking so much until coming back to Dotty's. The time spent with her preparing and cooking food is special. We talk about everything and nothing and put the world to rights. Surely life is made for living in kitchens? Food isn't just a necessity for existing, but an opportunity for sharing our time with loved ones. When there had been three of us in the kitchen, laughter had filled the house. A memory of mum, Nana and me dancing in the kitchen while cooking the roast, floods through me. From out of nowhere I'm crying for lost time. For days snatched, which I should have had with my mum with me. It wasn't fair. Life isn't fair. Is everyone going to die on me?

Unexpectedly, with no warning, the blackness that is depression jumps upon me. With the tick of a single second

I'm defeated. I fall to the floor. No thoughts. Just pain. Blackness. A wish to end it all.

My guardian angel swoops in at just that moment. As it's hard for her to reach for the floor she calls and calls until I respond and get to my feet, where Nana is able to wrap her arms around me and hold me tight. There is no need for words. We have been here many times before. Hush-hushing gently in my ear, she rocks me slowly until the anguish of loss and despair begins to fade. Dotty manages to usher me into the front room and onto the sofa. She wraps a throw around my shoulders and puts on the film Seven Brides for Seven Brothers. It's not to watch. It's just to have cheery background music as she helps to lift me back out of the mire.

I don't know what I would do without my Nana.

Chapter 8

BY WEDNESDAY, THANKFULLY, the upped dosage of anti-depressants has kicked in and I'm feeling calm and more myself. One day, I'm determined to be free of medication, but in the meantime I thank God for them. On the way to the meeting, Luke and I fall into easy conversation.

Luke patiently listens as I repeat everything I've already told him on the phone. I catch him turning his head ever so slightly to glance at me. His dark eyes are bouncing with life, his full lips curved in a half-smile. An urge to reach up and run my fingers through his short, dark hair rises up in me. I catch my breath; the strength of longing to touch his face is filling me, spreading within me like the opening of flower petals. I don't ever remember being this attracted to Roland. The thought of my deceased husband sobers me. I turn to look out the window and away from this person I fear is beginning to mean rather a lot.

"I hope this project will become everything you want it to be." His words ring with sincerity.

I turn back to look at him. "Thank you."

"I only have one reservation."

"What's that?"

"That you will move to Wales permanently, and we will be finished before we've started."

"I'm not planning on moving to Wales." Even though I respond immediately, something inside me is out of kilter, like maybe I do realize already that I'm be prepared to move if it means success for the project and therefore the children.

As if to reassure myself that I don't plan on moving, I add. "My home will always have to be close to Dotty. I couldn't live far away in case she ever needs me."

"I almost believe you."

Luke's words upset me, although I'm not a hundred per cent sure why. Before I can question him about it, the car slows down.

"I think this is it," he says nodding to a drive on the left before pulling into it.

"Yes, there's the sign," I say, pointing to a charming white painted board with flowers carved around the wooden edge.

Welcome to Munroe Farm

We pull into a graveled car park and look around at all the other cars.

"Looks like a well-attended meeting," says Luke.

I glance at my watch, it's 6.45 pm. "Everyone's early."

"Including us. Come on, let's go." Luke gets out of the car and starts walking around to my side. Déjà vu's ghost-like touch sends a shiver down my back making me jump out of the car before Luke can open the door. He's not my chauffeur anymore, he's my... my what? Friend? More than that, I'd be lying to myself if I said he was only a friend. I know I have to wait, let some water flow under that old bridge of life, but I also know, without doubt, that I want to be with him. That knowledge doesn't dispel any of the fear I have. To love someone is to lose them, right?

"You OK?"

Lord, but he's so keyed into my emotions it's scary. I 'umm' and nod.

"Welcome! So glad you could make it. I'm Jack." Jack steps back to allow us to enter into the huge barn-conversion, before offering Luke his hand.

I introduce them. "Jack, this is Luke. Luke, this is Jack."

Luke shakes his hand. Jack is a couple of inches taller, but Luke has a body-builder's physique. Out of the two I know whose arms I'd like to be in. The sudden thought makes me smile. Yes, I'd really like to have those muscly biceps wrapped around me. A warm glow creeps up my neck. Jack might be more traditionally handsome, but Luke is *all* man. I suddenly wish he was all *my* man. I slip my hand into his. He looks down at me in surprise and after the briefest moment firmly grips my hand as if he has no intention of ever letting it go.

"Come on through," says Jack. "I think nearly everyone is here. We're just having something to eat before we start, so please help yourself whenever you're ready. In the meantime, let me introduce you to Danielle who found us the perfect spot for our project."

We walk through into an airy crowded room with a high ceiling. Many people stop their talking and eating to smile and say hello as we pass through. We come to a halt by the side of a small group, who all turn to smile upon our arrival. "Danielle, this is the lady I told you about who is thinking of volunteering. Charity and Luke, this is Danielle our neighbor."

"Nice to meet you," I say holding out my hand to shake Danielle's. Instead of taking my hand she surprises me by throwing the largest smile and then leaning in to give me a firm, albeit brief, hug. Danielle is absolutely stunning with deep brown eyes, and long, straight brown hair. With perfect creamy skin and full lips she could easily have just walked off the front cover of Vogue magazine. To top it off she's slim, but somehow firmly built like she works out, strength both physical and mental oozes from her. I want to look at Luke to see if he is drowning in her gorgeous eyes but I daren't do it, in case he is.

"Pleased to meet you Luke," she says, offering him her hand. They shake and I'm unbelievably relieved she doesn't hug him. "This is my brother Aymon," she nods towards someone who is best described as a Jesus look-alike. Piercing light blue eyes, salt and pepper hair falling around his shoulders and moustache and beard to finish it off. It doesn't help my vision of him as a biblical character that he's wearing a hippy style, collarless multi-colored shirt that hangs loosely. He nods towards us and we nod back.

"This is another one of my brothers, Tristan." She nods towards a most handsome man standing next to Aymon. I can't help my right eyebrow lifting ever so slightly; it is obvious they must be adopted siblings. He exudes confidence and power. He's wearing suit trousers with a matching waist coat, under which lies the softest looking white shirt with emphasizes his dark skin to perfection. I'm literally blown away by how striking he is, and then I'm brought back to earth by a gentle squeeze of my hand from Luke!

"Nice to meet you all," I say trying to cover up the fact that I'd been gaping. "Are you all planning on helping out with this vision of Megan's and Jack's?"

"We are indeed, we plan to follow the pair of them around and be there for whatever is needed," answers Aymon.

"So, will you take a year off work or something?" Luke asks.

"As it happens we are all in-between jobs at the moment," replies Danielle. "Luckily, we are all financially secure, so if we take one or two years off, it will be fine."

"Lucky you," says Luke. I pick up a slight tinge of jealousy. It's my turn to squeeze his hand in reassurance.

"You really should help yourself to a drink and something to eat before we start," says Tristan. "Trust me, we never know how long these meetings will last."

We take his advice and head to the corner of the room where the buffet has been set up. After heartily enjoying some food, we have each just grabbed a drink of lemonade when Jack calls out for everyone to find a seat. We are in a large reception room, which I overheard someone mention was the venue for the marriage ceremonies for the wedding events the Munroes run. Chairs have been put out in rows, much like a church setting. We take seats about half-way back from the stage and get comfortable. I place my handbag under the seat. Inside my check book waits.

Megan takes the microphone from Jack and thanks everyone for coming. Then with the aid of a slide show, she begins to tell us all about their vision. By the time she's finished, I'm hooked. Without a shadow of a doubt, this is the project for Roland's money. Megan and Jack have a vision to take children and teenagers on holiday, to build their confidence and offer them a piece of joy where possible. To offer them two weeks holiday, free from worry and hunger as well as cost. The only thing required of the young people is to attend a service on Sunday morning. Everything else will be up to them. The charity board wants to hire sports coaches and event organizers to make sure the holidays are packed with as much outdoor action as possible. What they don't know is how best to convert the cottages, and how to fund the purchase and maintenance, along with the all year round salaries.

When she finishes the slide show and talk, Megan asks if anyone has any questions. Different people ask about different things. I wait until there is a lull, and then raise my hand.

"Yes, Charity?" I'm touched she knows my name. It fills me with confidence. Normally hating the limelight there would be no way I would get up and speak in front of people, but this project has emboldened me.

"If I was to donate a substantial amount of money that would ensure this project was able to take off, could we give the place a new name?"

Megan doesn't ask how much money. "What name did you have in mind?"

"My husband died last year. I would be using his inheritance to fund this, so if we could swap the name of the cottage setting to Byron's Haven I would be delighted to donate not only two million pounds, but also my services as an architect and all round dogs-body." There is a sharp intake of breath around the room at the mention of the amount of money.

Jack steps up to Megan and whispers in her ear. She nods then looks at the crowd. "We have all our charity board members present. Can we please have a vote for a venue name change?" There's a murmur of approval around the room.

"All in favor?" Jack asks.

I glance around the room and do a quick count; eight people have raised their hands, including Danielle and her two brothers and a vicar.

"No need to ask if anyone is against then," declares Jack, "we are all in favor."

An explosion of joy erupts in my chest. There is no other way to describe it. I feel high as a kite, to the extent I almost believe I can fly! I drop back into my seat and look at Luke. Aware of my gaze he turns his head slowly and looks at me. He's sad. I'm about to ask what's up when Megan announces the end of formalities, and that now is a time to get to know everyone and to talk about how they see it all coming together. We are instantly surrounded by people wanting to ask if I have a vision on how to convert the cottages.

Snowed under by questions, I would normally collapse under pressure, but sheer joy urges me back to my feet to discuss ideas and plans with complete strangers.

I'm not sure how long I've been talking, but I suddenly realize I'm shattered. My throat is really dry from at least an hour's conversation. I notice a lot of people have already gone. I glance around the room looking for Luke. Unrealistic panic that he might have got bored and left rises up in me. As if sensing my distress, he is suddenly by my elbow.

"Here," he says handing me a drink of water.

"Thanks, you're a life saver."

He stays beside me as we talk to the last few people still here. Eventually it is just us and the Munroes. I take my check book out of my bag.

"I'd like to give you the money now, so you can buy the property before someone else snaps it up. I've been to Beddgelert for the day a few years ago. We went for a six-hour walk along the river and then up in the hills, finishing the day with fish and chips in the loveliest of restaurants in the village. It is one of the most beautiful spots I have ever seen. I can hardly believe a part of it is up for sale."

"Thank you," says Jack. "However, it would be best if you did a bank transfer, and only do that after you have spoken to a lawyer. You are about to hand over a very large sum of money."

I look up at Luke. He nods in agreement. I put the check book away.

"You should get your lawyer to check out our charity and to clarify with you that we are above board. Also, Danielle and her brothers donated half a million last week, and the owners of the property have accepted that as a deposit until we can raise the rest. We had no idea the rest would come so quickly, praise God!"

"Will it be alright if I go and visit the property?"

"Yes of course, we'll give you the caretaker's number and you can let her know you're coming."

"I just need to be there to take measurements and get a feel of everything before I start on my draft drawings."

"Maybe we could say a quick prayer together before we go home?" I look at Luke in surprise. I really wish he hadn't said that.

"That would be wonderful," replies Megan.

I suddenly feel like an ice maiden, totally frozen and cold. I don't pray, and if I did I certainly wouldn't do it out loud in front of people. The four of us hold hands and close our eyes. Jack opens with a prayer of thanks. When he has finished Luke prays for the Lord's blessing on the project and vision. As if aware that I wouldn't be praying, Megan refrains from joining in. I'm grateful to not be made to feel like the odd one out. I wish I could believe as much as these people did, but I just can't. Life is too full of pain to have been created by a God that is supposed to be loving and compassionate. I know I often raise my eyes to the sky and whisper thank you, but I'm sure it is a more childlike habit than a belief.

Chapter 9

OVER THE LAST FEW WEEKS I have put a few pounds on. I look better. My face isn't so gaunt, and I have to admit the fat has puffed out the skin taking away the tiny wrinkles that have crept around my eyes and lips. Cosmetics used to do a marvelous job of making me look like a beauty queen, but now I feel like I can be me without makeup, fresh and natural looking.

Looking in the mirror I'm pensive, unaware I'm chewing my lower lip. There's no avoiding it, going out for a meal with Luke tonight is officially a date. I feel so nervous. I have no idea where he is taking me and I don't know what to wear. Nearly all of my clothes have been donated to charity shops. I've kept a lot of my every day wear, jeans, tops etc, but nearly all my evening clothes have gone.

Although, this morning started off cold and frosty, the temperatures had slowly risen with the sun and clouds playing tic-tac-toe. Too cold for a nice dress, I opt for smart pants and a soft blouse. After applying a small amount of eye-shadow, mascara and a touch of lipstick I sit back and inspect myself once more. Luke has seen me dressed to kill. Done up to-the-nines and comfortable enough in my looks to mix with the rich and famous. What will he think when he sees me like this? Will he think I've not made an effort for him? For a moment I'm nearly tempted to start over again, changing both my clothes and putting on a full set of makeup. However, a quick glance at my watch shows me I don't have enough time. Great! Just as I am then.

Prompt as usual, Luke rings the bell at 8 pm.

"Have a good time, dear," says Nana giving me a kiss before I leave. I have a warm coat on, which hides my outfit. I wish, I wish, I wish I had put something prettier on. Luke is in a suit and looks drop-dead-gorgeous.

Luke's gaze lingers on my eyes for a long time. "You look beautiful," he whispers before taking my arm and leading me to the car. I can't help a sigh of relief as I get in.

There is comfortableness between us now, and we instantly fall into chatter. "So how are things progressing? Where you up to?"

I can't help sighing at his question. Things since Roland's death seem to have been non-stop. I've forgotten how many meetings with the lawyers I've had it's that many. The money from the sale of the house and all the antiques, plus some of my larger pieces of jewelry has all gone through. I've now got, after paying a jaw-dropping amount to the lawyers, two million and twenty thousand pounds in the bank. The transfer to the trust goes through tomorrow which will leave me the smallest amount I've had in my personal bank account since marrying. I really hope the hotels sell soon. For the first time since offering the money to the project, vulnerability has become my second skin. I've put aside buying a house until the hotels sell. I've also had to release Judith. It really upset me, but she was so understanding, and after staying at her house for about three hours we had hugged tightly before I left.

My heart beats like the clunk of a grandfather clock. Each tick to tock swings my emotions from outright terror at being broke to indescribable joy at giving it all away. The range of emotions and the constant battle going on within my thoughts is quite honestly enough to send me to bed for a week. Like Nana says, I'm at the beginning of a whole new life.

"The money is being transferred on Monday."

"And you're still sure this is what you want to do?"

"Yes. I never felt that any of Roland's things were mine anyway. I believed I was merely a passenger along for the ride."

"Do you miss him?"

I turn in my seat to look at Luke. His eyes are firmly fixed on the road ahead. His hands hold tight to the steering wheel. I try to choose my words carefully.

"Roland was a force to be reckoned with. Everything always felt like a whirlwind with him. Things were loud and bombastic. He dragged me all over the world in the early years. It was wonderful at first. He made me feel special and loved. I saw some tremendous places and I'll never forget our safari in Kenya, it was too amazing for words. But he changed. The cocaine was the end of our relationship really; nothing I did could stop him. I felt like such a failure as I watched him waste away before my eyes. Not his body so much as his personality. I guess you know what he got up to?"

I see the corner of Luke's eyes twitch, it's all the answer I need. "The last couple of years were lonely. So, yes I do miss him. That is the Roland I met at university. But I don't miss what my life had turned into in the end." After a moment of silence I ask Luke a question. "Do you still miss your wife?"

"I do."

My heart slumps a little.

"I don't think you ever stop missing a person you loved. It does get easier though. I don't believe that time heals your wounds. I believe it's more a case that you learn to live with it better. Tanya was such a vibrant person, the life and soul of every part of my day. She believed in experiencing life and enjoying it to the full. She jam-packed our every weekend with something to do. It was tiring sometimes, but it was also a lot of fun."

"She sounds lovely."

"She was. She was a real darling. It was hard at first matching someone who loved life so much with death. It didn't seem fair. Then slowly I began to realize that it was wonderful how she packed her life with activities. Because she made each day count, it seemed like she'd lived a full life. As she didn't have many years, all I can think is thank goodness she did all that she did when she had the chance."

How could I ever believe I could compete with her? I'm a depressive. I wish I was a joyful and energetic person, but in truth I can be quite the opposite.

Luke changes the subject. "So you stocked up on toilet roll yet?"

"What?"

"The panic buying? I've heard there's no toilet roll left in the shops. Just wondering if you were able to stock up before the shops sold out."

I chuckle. "Why? Do you need some?"

Luke laughs. "No. Mum and Dad do a monthly shop at Costco. As it happens they'd done a shop last week so we're good for a month at least. I hear the shelves are emptying quickly though, with people panic buying."

"I don't get it. Why do you think they're stockpiling toilet roll?"

"Wartime mentality? Toilet roll was considered a luxury item not an everyday item, until well after World War Two."

"There's not many people left who remember that though."

"You'd be surprised."

"So if the shops were to be empty for a while, what couldn't you live without?"

"Blimey, that's easy. Potatoes."

"Potatoes?"

"Yep."

"Why?"

"It must be the Irish in me. My granddad was Irish. My mum looked after him in his last few years after he moved in with us. We had to have potatoes at every meal. Not chips though, he didn't like them at all."

"Every meal?"

"Yep, and mountains of them. Boiled, mashed, gratin, roast, but his all-time favorite was colcannon. He would have been happy if all you'd put on his plate was a pile of colcannon."

"So it's more to do with the memory of mashed potato mixed with cabbage than just having potato?"

"Could be, but I do love potatoes."

I'm delighted when he doesn't drive us too far and we end up at my favorite Italian restaurant.

"Thank you for bringing me here, I love this place," I tell him as we go in.

"I know," he winks back.

Of course, driving me around for a few years would reveal my favorite haunts. Roland hadn't been fond of Italian food, so my memories of this place are not tinged with sadness as I used to come with ladies from my old neighborhood.

"La signora Byron, benvenuta," says the maître d' as we enter.

"Giovanni, how wonderful to see you!"

We air-kiss each other's cheeks three times before he lets go of me and stands back. He should have retired a long time ago, but he's told me often he doesn't yet trust his young boy (forty-eight year old Antonio) to run things to his wishes.

"My deepest sympathies for your loss, I was molto triste when I heard."

There is a lump in my throat. Why is it that a waiter's condolences can feel more heart-felt than any of Roland's acquaintances?

"Where would you like us to sit, Giovanni?" asks Luke, taking my elbow.

Giovanni's water-filled eyes, in his darkly tanned lined face, look up at Luke. Forever a businessman, he instantly smiles. "Come this way, I have saved our best table for you, of course."

"Grazie," says Luke, as Giovanni hands us a menu each before leaving.

Luke looks at me. "Are you alright?"

To be honest, the sudden sympathy caught me by surprise and it has been a battle not to cry. Desperate not to have runny mascara I have bashed the sadness deep down.

"Yes, thank you. It just caught me unawares."

"Do you want to go home?"

A wave of loving affection floods through me. Luke is too good for me. I've never met anyone so considerate before. I shake my head. "No, I'm fine. Plus I'm longing for some spaghetti carbonara!"

Italian music is piped through the restaurant at just the right level, so it's there soothing the silences but not that loud as you can't hear each other. The smell of garlic and other food, floods through from the kitchen making my stomach grumble, demanding something soon. I bite the end of a grissini stick as I listen to Luke tell me stories from his youth. His large hands are twirling his glass of Chianti round as he chats away. I'm listening, but I'm also wondering how long it will take before I will feel comfortable enough to be his girlfriend. This is a date; does that mean I am already his girlfriend? I wonder what he thinks.

Luke has stopped talking and is smiling at me. I've missed something. Shock must be clear to see, I feel like a deer caught in the headlights.

"I asked… do you think you will live in Wales now you know how involved in the project you're going to be?"

"I've been asking myself the same question. I think I might see if I can split my time between here and Wales. I've checked. It's two and half hours away if I take the direct route through the country roads, or just over two hours if I take the longer freeway route."

"So I've not lost you yet then."

On impulse, I reach out placing my hand over his, which is now lying on the table-top. "I hope you never lose me."

I see relief emanating from him. "You know I…"

A waiter suddenly appears with my pasta and Luke's steak.

"Hold that thought," I tell him. I have a sudden dread he's about to tell me he loves me, and I'm not ready for *that*. "If I don't eat now I think the whole restaurant with hear my stomach!"

The waiter puts the plates down and asks if we need anything else.

"The peppermill please," I answer. As he turns away, I lift my glass. "Here's to tomorrow, and all the days that follow."

"I'll drink to that."

"Are you sure?"

I take hold of Luke's hand and pull him into the house. "It's only coffee not an invitation to frolic. Besides, Nana is still up. See, the lights are on."

We take our shoes off in the hallway and hang our coats on the coat-stand.

I push open the front room door. "Hi, Nana."

Dotty turns to face us. Something is wrong. She is sitting on the edge of the sofa, her back straight, her hands clasped tight together on her lap. "I've recorded the 10 pm news for you. You have to see what's happening. It's awful, just awful."

I rush to sit beside her, and nod towards the arm chair for Luke. "What's happened?"

"It's this virus, oh it's terrible. Watch. Just watch this." Dotty puts the remote back on the table after getting the screen to where she wants it. She pulls a large white handkerchief out of her pocket and blows her nose loudly. Luke and I are glued to the screen as we watch a news reporter walk around a hospital in Lombardy, Italy.

"We have been overwhelmed by a tsunami of patients," a translator says after listening to a doctor, who is completely covered in protective clothing and both a cloth face mask and a plastic visor. The doctor continues talking in Italian. I wait, shock and anxiety turning my blood cold, for the translator to continue.

The doctor indicates for the recording crew to follow him through the hospital. Patients fill every bed. Ventilators bleep as they pump oxygen down tubes into the patient's lungs, taking over the breathing function, replacing lungs that are failing to work on their own. A pain in my chest starts rising. This is dreadful, horrible, worse than anything I have ever seen. The lump in my throat is so hard I fear it might choke me. Release from it comes only when I give in and allow tears to flow freely.

After a tour of the overcrowded hospital, the reporter and crew go outside. She pulls off her mask to talk to the camera. "People must have thought they were on the ship Titanic, for they have been out eating and drinking, even dancing and partying. A last hurrah before the ship sinks maybe? As the death toll mounts, governments must take action. Something must be done to slow this pandemic. As Dr. Russo said… 'United Kingdom beware' for *we will* be hit harder than this."

After blowing my nose, I look over at Luke. "Why will we be hit harder?"

"Because the Italian government introduced preventatives to the virus spreading straight away, while our government is dragging its feet apparently."

After we switch the television off I make some hot chocolate. We sit around the kitchen table trying to digest what we've just seen and heard.

"Don't lots of people die each year of normal flu anyway? Isn't this just worse because it's like everyone is getting it at the same time?" I look between them.

Luke answers. "I believe this is going to be much worse than the flu. I was listening to the radio the other day where some expert or other was comparing this outbreak to the Spanish flu of 1918. The thing that encourages me is, that pandemic naturally exhausted itself within two years."

"You don't think this will last that long do you?" I ask, shocked.

Luke takes my hand. "Let's just wait and see. No need to panic now before we know what's going to happen. Dotty did you have your flu jab last year?"

"Yes, I had it at the end of October."

"I don't think it would do any harm if you stayed at home as much as possible, reduce the risk of catching it." Luke says.

"I refuse to live in fear young man. Besides, I will be going home to Heaven the day my Father calls me and not a day before."

"I would prefer that day to be later rather than sooner, Nana. Maybe we could use a bit of caution?"

"We'll see. Anyway, I'm calling it a day and going to bed. I found that news quite distressing and I'm exhausted."

She surprises me when after kissing my forehead, she leans over and kisses Luke's too. "Goodnight you two."

"Night-night, Nana."

"Good night Mrs. Williams, sleep well."

"Tut tut young man, the name's Dotty."

"Night Dotty." They exchange sincere smiles. My heart warms knowing Luke has Nana's seal of approval.

A short while after she has gone Luke takes both my hands in his. "She's a tough old bird, she'll be fine. We'll look out for her."

"The reporter said the highest numbers affected are those in those who are over eight-five."

"How old is Dotty?" Luke asks.

My voice catches as I give the answer. "Eighty-eight."

"She'll be alright, Charity."

Fear throws buckets of anxiety at me. Tears stream down my cheeks, a never-ending flow of salt-filled stress. Luke gets up and fetches the kitchen roll from the counter. He tears off a sheet and uses it to mop up my waterfall.

I turn my face up towards him. Thankfulness replaces fear. In this moment I know that I have two people who truly love me. Two wonderful people, how lucky am I?

My eyes must have reflected the sudden rush of love I feel for him, because Luke bends down, cups my face in his hands and plants a very tender kiss upon my lips.

Chapter 10

AFTER ARRANGING TO MEET the caretaker I jump into the car with much enthusiasm. It's Tuesday morning on a bright spring-fresh day. I can't wait to see what the cottages look like on the inside and figure out what I can do to update them and hopefully fit more beds in.

Mrs. Evans comes out of the first cottage when I pull through the open wooden gates two hours later, and drive into the communal driveway. Dark rain clouds hover low, but even so I'm in awe of such a beautiful location. The rolling hills behind the cottages are awash with different colors. Red heather squashes between splashes of emerald greens and flourishes of gray rocks. It's simply stunning. Families and children coming here for holidays from the Manchester area are sure to have an amazing time.

"Hello," I call, as the middle-aged, rotund brunette makes her way towards me.

"Bore da," she calls back. "Croeso... welcome to Beddgelert." Her slow, honey-toned accent is like music. We shake hands firmly. Eye-to-eye contact tells me I'm dealing with someone honest and open.

After the tour of the five cottages I'm rather deflated.

"You don't like them?" asks Mrs. Evans in her sing-song voice.

"No, quite the opposite, I think they're perfect. They're also in excellent condition, you can tell they're well looked after."

"I see. I got the impression that you were disappointed, like."

"I am a bit. I didn't realize they were so modern, I was hoping to be able to work on and improve them. As it happens, there's not much I can do." I have taken tons of photos and measurements to go over things once I get home, but in my heart I know these modern cottages don't need anything doing. I feel somewhat bereft, if I'm honest. I'd so been looking forward to working on this project.

After lunch in the delightful Café Glandwr, I hop back in the car and hit the road before the storm threatening overhead hits hard. After joining the main road, I use the hands-free and call Megan to give her my initial feedback.

"Well," she says when I've finished reporting, "we might not need your skills with design, but you did also say you were happy to be a general dogs-body if I remember rightly?"

"Yes, that's true."

"So why not join us in some of our ventures? We help out at several youth clubs and children's care homes. We're also involved in supplying food to those who need it through a food-bank society. We also help out at soup-kitchens whenever we can."

"Gosh you're busy. You do all that on top of running a wedding venue?"

"There are ten of us in our charity, and between us we help out as much as possible. Reverend Bowen is instrumental in pointing us all in the right direction, I don't think we would do half the things we do without him. Plus we hire in staff when the weddings take place, which isn't very often as yet as we are quite new and still building up our reputation."

Just then lightning flashes through the dark skies in front of me, and I can't help shivering. It's gone so dark it's like night-time, instead of afternoon. "I think I'd best get off the phone so I can concentrate. It looks like I'm about to drive through a right storm."

"Well, have a think about what I said and if you're interested give me a call. The youngsters from the homes will be the first people we take to Wales so if you want to help with the trips it might be good if you came along a couple of times and got to meet the kids."

"I will do, I'll call you soon. Bye for now."

I can't hear Megan's farewell as a crack of thunder deafens me. I hit the call-stop button on the steering wheel and hold on tight. The first drops of rain hit the car like stones. The windscreen wipers go onto full mode straight away, but it's still hard to see. I pull into the slow lane on the freeway, dropping my speed to fifty miles an hour. A car races passed me, its spray drenching my car and temporarily obscuring my view of the road ahead. "Idiot," I yell at the driver.

After fifteen minutes of downpour, the tension in me is making me ill. I've got to stop, but I've not seen a turning off since the rain started. "Please God, I need a service station to pull into and wait out the worst. I don't think I can drive much further." As two trucks go hurtling past, covering the car with spray once more, I begin to panic. I hate storms. From an early age, thunder and lightning have struck fear in me. Many a time as a young girl, during a night storm I had run into Nana's room to let her protective arms keep me safe. Tight muscles in my neck are beginning to send shooting pains through me. I have to stop. "God please, get me safely to the next service station, and I promise to go to church with Nana on Sunday." After twenty seconds, I add. "For a month!" Did He hear me? Who knows? What I do know is in that precise moment the rain begins to ease. Within another five minutes, I'm driving out of it into clear blue skies. "Crazy British weather!" And hey presto, guess what? There's a service station. Thinking the clouds might be blowing this way, and if I stop then I'll still be under them, I decide to drive on and get home as quickly as possible.

I don't know why I'm nervous, but I am. I feel slightly sick, something akin to interview nerves. Megan and Jack wave at me as I get out of the car. Come on you stupid woman, you can do this! Well fingers crossed I can.

"Hi," I call as I walk towards them. We're on the driveway of a house in Stockport. It looks much like all the other houses around. It's detached and set back from the road by a longish drive. Once upon a time this would have been a house for someone very well off. Now, the surrounding area of Stockport has sprung up and enveloped what once was a quiet area. Still, an impressive building by size and structure, it was however showing signs of age and crying out for a good dose of maintenance. It was now known as Thornhill Children's Home.

The Munroes' smiles are warm and welcoming. I have no idea why I'm so nervous. I've had several Face-time meetings with Megan in the last few days. When I'd mentioned that I loved cooking, she had suggested that I might want to come one afternoon and give three of the girls here a cookery lesson whilst preparing their evening meal. I'd never taught anyone anything in my life and I wasn't a hundred per cent sure I could do it, but here I am.

I'd emailed the recipe for chicken and broccoli bake to Megan, and they had gone shopping and bought all the ingredients. So, armed with several shopping bags, we go in. I can't help looking around; I am pleasantly surprised - it very much resembles a normal family home. A high ceiling and lots of tall windows fill the house with light and a sense of openness. The front room and dining room have had the inner wall knocked out to create one large space.

"Joe," Megan calls out as we walk down the hall and into the kitchen.

A lanky middle-aged man appears. His freckled face an expression of seriousness. "Hi," he nods towards us. He's wringing his long thin fingers together and is obviously worked up.

"Everything alright?" asks Jack.

"Maisy's done *it* again. I've been waiting for you to arrive so I can drive to hospital and fill in the forms. The ambulance took her away two hours ago but there was no one free to come and relieve me. Joanne is coming on duty at 5 pm; will you be OK until she arrives, if I go now?"

With that one sentence I am fully reminded that despite the fact this might look like a normal home, it's not.

"Sure thing," answers Jack, "Who's in?"

"Only Katy, Lou and Simone," Joe answers while putting his coat on and lifting a set of keys off a hook on the wall.

"Sarah and Jane are on a school trip; their teacher isn't dropping them off until after 6 pm."

"Where are the girls now?"

"All in their rooms, normally we don't encourage them to coop themselves up but well… today turned out not to be a normal day."

"You get going," says Megan, "we'll stay until we're not needed."

"Thanks." With a wave, Joe shoots out the back door.

"It?" I ask when he's gone.

"Maisy has attempted to take her life half a dozen times now," Jack answers while putting the bags on the table.

The sadness of it knocks me for six. "How old is she?"

"Seventeen," answers Jack.

"I'll go and fetch the girls down," say Megan.

I start unloading the bags with Jack. "That's terrible," I whisper.

"She's a troubled soul that's for sure. She's received her list of steps for moving out of here and unfortunately, she's not taken it very well. We're praying something positive comes into her life."

I don't know what to say. 'Poor girl' is on repeat in my mind.

Katy, Lou and Simone follow Megan into the kitchen. Katy I'm told is fifteen. Both Lou and Simone are sixteen. Katy is tiny, mouse-brown hair and a timid voice. Lou barks when she laughs and has me in fits. Simone is a Goth and everything is black. She is very attached to her cell which we soon learn is impossible for her to put down. I catch a picture of the boy she is messaging and shiver at his hard looking face.

Megan and Jack leave me to the cooking lesson and go to work cleaning the house. I'm impressed with them and their willingness to clean anything, including the outside drain that we learn is blocked yet again.

Talking to the young girls gets easier as we go along. They watch and participate with interest, which builds my confidence.

"We normally only get microwave bakes," blurts Simone after a while of watching from the side-lines.

"They can be OK," I answer, "but there's nothing quite like home-cooked food, it tastes so much better. They say food is the way to a man's heart you know." All three girls are attentive after that.

On the drive home I am full of joy. The girls seem genuinely to like me and for some unexplainable reason that fills me with happiness. I can honestly say I'd never felt more satisfaction than when Katy had asked if I was going to come back and teach them something else to cook. I've loved my first introduction to the world of volunteering, and I can't wait to do more.

When I get home there's an email from Trevor & Cornelius. There's been an offer for the hotels. It's below the asking price but I'm just happy for them to sell. I email back straight away instructing them to accept the offer. An email pings back to me the following morning, confirming go ahead pending a due-diligence audit by their accountants.

Chapter 11

LOOKING AT THE EMAIL IS LIKE FACING the Grim Reaper. Trepidation skulks around the corners of my mind, shadows of unknown fear, otherwise called dread. I read it for about the tenth time just to make sure I'm not hallucinating and the contents, from some person I've never heard of before but who works at Trevor & Cornelius, is really there.

> *Dear Mrs. Byron*
>
> *We have called you but been unable to reach you. Could you please call the office at your earliest convenience? We are afraid that the news on the due diligence is not positive.*
>
> *With regret, we inform you that your husband's business is showing a deficit. The auditors have discovered financial discrepancies and a total of eight hundred thousand owing to Lloyd's Bank. The prospective buyers have confirmed their original offer no longer stands. They have however, showed a willingness to take the business on at a rate of five pence in the pound. After all charges, including ours, this will result in a payment due to you of forty thousand or there about.*
>
> *We cordially invite you to consider this offer, which we believe in the current*

climate and uncertain times to be generous and fair. Should you decide to accept it, this will prevent the company from going bankrupt, and although appearing somewhat negative to yourself, this will however prevent a scandal involving your late husband's name.

It just can't be. It just can't. How can everything be gone – just like that? Am I being ripped off? Or has the mixture of Roland's account draining and Covid collided with catastrophic consequences?

I should call them, but I feel so sick I don't think I can talk. If I had known this was going to happen I wouldn't have given all the money away. How stupid was I to give it away before I had sold the business? Idiot. Idiot. Idiot. Angry tears of self-pity roll down my face. From riches to rags in a matter of weeks! Oh, OK, maybe not rags. But I had thought I was going to be comfortable for life and now I have what, maybe two or three years' worth of money?

I start pacing. Think, think. What do I do? Before I even realize what I'm doing, the cell phone is in my hands and I'm calling Luke.

"Hello beautiful."

Hot air floods out of me in a dragon-sized sigh. How is possible with just two words he can make me feel better? "Hi." I sit down on the sofa, leaning back on the soft cushions.

"Got to be quick, I'm just between jobs. Are you alright?"

"Just had some bad news, I thought, well I thought, actually I don't know what I was thinking. I guess I just wanted to talk to you."

"Oh, babes, I'm sorry. What's happened?"

I fill him in quickly on the latest email. "What do you think I should do?"

"My first thought is you should call your other lawyer, Sebastian is it?"

"Yes."

"Run everything by him and see what he says. I know this seems like a terrible blow to you Charity, but at least you have some money coming in. It will hold you together until you find your feet. I'm not a money guru but my every instinct is saying you should take the money before they retract their second offer. Things aren't looking very good with this virus. There are some prophets of doom and gloom predicting that a world-wide economic crash is about to hit. They might be wrong, but if they're right, the small amount of money in your bank account is better than none."

"You're right. It's just I was already spending the money, planning what else I could do for the Wales project and buying myself a house. It's all gone now." I can't help the self-pity that rises inside me or the lump in my throat that's making it hard to talk.

"You have to remember that you're still in a far better position than millions and millions of people around the world."

"Gosh, you sound like my mum! Eat your veg, there's millions and millions of starving children in the world!"

"Sorry."

"No, it's fine. I needed to hear it out loud. Of course I'll be fine. Money doesn't make you happy; I for one know that to be true. I've got Nana, and you, and we're all healthy. I'm lucky, I know."

"It doesn't mean you can't be disappointed, but you're right. Where it counts, you and me babes, we're rich."

A heart-warming chuckle comes out of me. I think I love this man. Gosh what did I just say? Get a grip. "So are we still on for tomorrow night then?"

"Wild horses couldn't keep me away. Pick you up at seven."

"OK. See you tomorrow then."

"Bye babe, and be strong, you'll be alright, you'll see."

Fear is contagious. My heart is beating slightly faster than normal. Goodness knows how Nana's coping. A nervous trill runs through my adrenalin akin to excitement. Yet there is nothing to be excited about, in fact quite the opposite. I guess I must only have been halfheartedly listening to the news, because now that I'm standing in front of an empty supermarket aisle it's a shock. How accustomed we've become to having everything we need right at our fingers, exactly when we need it. I'd planned to cook pasta with tuna fish sauce for tea. The tuna, mushrooms, crème fraîche, tomatoes and basil sit in the shopping trolley. However, there isn't any pasta in sight. It just feels wrong. At no time in my life have I ever not been able to walk into a shop and get what I need, or just plain fancy.

An inexplicable urge rises up in me and I want to join the panic buying. Maybe we should get long-life stuff like tins of soup and corned beef; they don't go off. What about tinned milk and coffee? I turn to Nana, about to spurt out our need to fill our trolley to overflowing when I spot her 'look'.

"Let's get some puff pastry if they have any, and if they don't we'll make short crust when we get home. We'll have Russian Fish Pie instead," she says taking hold of the trolley and turning around. There's no stress on her face and no fear in her speech. What's wrong with me? Why on earth would I want to join in with the panic? I'd heard on the news that the large supermarkets are saying that their warehouses are full and there's no need to panic buy, so why did I want to join in with it so much? As we walk back to the fridge section, I ponder on parts of the world where scarcity is a common thing and shudder. How blessed are we to live in a country with such abundant wealth. I can't imagine what it must be like to live in places that are poor where the shop shelves are perpetually empty. Despite my intention to take the higher ground, remain noble and not panic buy, just as we're nearing the tills I spot an abandoned nine-pack of toilet roll that someone has left on the end of the aisle. My resolve diminishes. The pack is quickly snapped up and dropped into our trolley.

"What?" I say when I spot Nana's raised eyebrows. "You can never have too much, can you?"

I've got to be honest and say this wasn't the kind of date I thought Luke had in mind when he asked me to come out with him tonight. Luckily, he had briefed me to come in comfortable clothes and flat shoes. So here I am in my jeans, t-shirt and trainers complete with plastic apron, gloves and face mask standing behind a counter dishing out food.

The Stockport soup-kitchen is full to capacity. There are two other women helping serve and an army of about ten volunteers in the kitchen, including Luke who is equipped like me and standing over a pile of dishes at the sink. I hear him laughing with the guys beside him and my stomach flips. There's no doubt this man - who I've known for years without knowing at all - is working his way into my heart.

"Would you like cabbage with that?" I ask a pock-marked, greasy-haired lanky lad, after putting cottage pie on his plate. He grins at me. Missing and blackened teeth draw my attention. I guess he's been on the streets for a while then.

"Yep love, fill it up." His smile is broad, though his eyes are haunting and sad.

"Sure thing," I answer, piling his plate high.

I'm shocked at how many people have come for a free meal. Lots of them are obviously regulars as the volunteers know their names and banter is goodhearted and full of caring. This building is only forty-five minutes away from the mansion I used to live in. I shudder. How could I have not known this place was here? How could I have lived without noticing the homeless and those in poverty? Shame flicks through my emotions on more than one occasion. In the end all I can say to myself is at least I'm here now. If only my eyes had been open when I was loaded, how much would I have been able to help?

I reel backwards as an overwhelming stink assaults my nose.

"No cabbage for me," says a small, rotund woman with crazy-wire red hair. She looks like she's just had an electric shock. My eyes are smarting from the smell but I pull myself together and smile.

"Enjoy your cottage pie," I say handing her a plate.

When there's a lull in the queue, another volunteer leans close and whispers. "You do get used to the smell, and Rosie doesn't come in every day. She walks great distances so only comes in when she's around Stockport."

"You'd think in this day and age we'd be able to house everyone," I whisper back.

"I used to think that. I did a lot of campaigning to get the homeless off the streets a few years back. Trouble is the number of homeless just keeps going up and up. Goodness knows what's going to happen when this depression caused by Covid kicks in. I dread to think how many people are going to lose their homes."

It was a sobering thought, one that settled into my psyche and took root.

"So, how did you find your first trip to the soup-kitchen?" Luke asks as he's driving me home.

"It was an eye-opener."

"Would you want to come back with me again?"

"Lord, yes!"

Luke chuckles, throwing me a quick sideways glance. "You liked it that much, eh?"

"I'm ashamed it's a world I've never entered before, but it is one that now I've found it I want to stay. Everyone was so cheerful and polite, weren't they?"

"Everyone except Swearing Simon," laughs Luke.

"Oh yeah, forgot about him for a moment, gosh but his language is blue."

"They don't even know they're swearing most of them, it's just part of their everyday conversation. If you can get over that and the odd smell you'll do just fine."

"I was talking to a young lad called Tom. He was only seventeen and has been on the streets for a year already. I really had to fight the urge to take him home with me and offer him a hot shower and a bed to sleep in for the night."

Luke reaches over and places a hand on my knee. "The thing is we can't take them all home. So we do what we can, which I know feels like next to nothing, but a hot meal is vital no matter how small it looks. Lots of them come for the chat too; some even say the company is worth more than the food to them. We do what we can, and we campaign for more government help."

We fall into silence for a while after that. There is no getting away from the fact that my life has been a total blessing compared to some other people.

I glance at Luke as he drives the last part of the journey. Although, sadness drifts over me sometimes like spindrift from a monstrous swash, being in the soup-kitchen this evening has filled me with joy and thankfulness for all I have. This happiness I know will prevent me from sinking under the giant sea swell of depression. I will don my sailor's cap and sail the seven seas, ahoy, me hearties I have the joy of giving in me old heart, no returning to the desert island for me!

"You coming in for a drink? It's only 10.30." I ask Luke as we pull up outside Dotty's house.

"Best not, I've got a very early start tomorrow. Let me walk you to the door." We get out and as we approach the entrance Luke takes my hand. Outside the door we turn to face each other.

"Mum has asked if you would like to join us for lunch this Sunday."

"Oh!" Red flames dance upon the embers of my cheeks.

"You don't have to come, it's just they've heard so much about you they'd really like to meet you."

"I'd love to come. I just get nervous with new people, that's all."

"You'll love my mum and dad, everyone does. You've got nothing to worry about."

"I'm sure I will. It's more a case of will I pass muster really."

Luke cups my face in his hands and turns it upwards to look at him. He's got this really soft, mushy type smile on his face and his eyes are twinkling, reflecting the street lamp.

"They'll love you," he whispers before leaning in to gently brush his lips against mine. Fireworks instantly explode within me. My stomach flips somersaults. Adolescent crush mixes with angst and wobbly knees. To be honest, I can't ever remember behaving like this before.

He straightens up and with the tips of his fingers brushes my hair off my face. I kind of want to surrender right now, let this passion inside me be released.

"I'll pick you up about two," he says, stepping back from me with obvious reluctance.

"You don't have to do that. I can drive over, just text me the address."

"OK, will do. Night."

"Night, Luke."

Nana and I are sobbing. "Well, that puts my life into perspective," I snuffle, then blow my nose. My heart is hurting so badly for the poor young nurse we've just seen on the television.

Critical care nurse Dawn Bilbrough from York, has just uploaded a video of herself in full breakdown. She'd been working an impossibly long shift and was heading home for a short break. She'd stopped at the shops to buy herself something for dinner but all the shelves were bare. *'Just stop it!'* she cried to the camera on her cell. Her emotional appeal touched many people because apparently she'd been inundated with offers of food. But the sad thing is it should never have happened. The shelves shouldn't have been bare. I'm choked on the sadness I feel for her.

What does it matter if I've lost so much money? Seriously, seriously, what does it matter? Human decency, kindness and thoughtfulness are worth more than all the gold in the world. We can't eat gold, or diamonds. I'm crushed with what is happening and the only thing I know for sure is, if I had inherited a lot of money from Roland's estate I would be giving it all away now anyway. Nana and I have a hug, something we've been doing a lot of recently. The comfort that comes from embracing someone is hard to describe. I just know her arms fill my soul with peace.

Chapter 12

BUTTERFLIES FLIP AROUND MY INSIDES like nobody's business as I reach up and press the bell. I lift the huge bunch of flowers I've brought up in front of my face. Why I think I can hide, I just don't know.

"They're beautiful, but you really shouldn't have."

I lower the flowers and grimace at Luke. "They're not for you as you well know. This is, though." I lift up a bottle of rosé.

"Thanks beautiful, come on in." Heat brims under my cheeks. I believe I'm a far cry from stunning, but each time he calls me beautiful I feel special. He places one hand behind my back and guides me into the kitchen, which I quickly realize is the hub and heart of the household.

"These are for you, Mum," Luke says offering her the flowers.

She ignores them completely. Instead, she charges straight for me and engulfs me in a massive bear-hug. "Now, let me see you," she says holding onto my shoulders but taking a step back. "My, you certainly are as delightful as our boy said. Welcome to the Smith household, and thank you for the flowers, although you really shouldn't have bothered."

"Come on woman, out the way, let me say hello." Luke's mum steps back and his dad steps forward. For a moment I thought he was going to hug me too, but he seems to change his mind at the last moment and instead offers me his hand. "Hi, I'm Dave. Nice to meet you."

"Hi," I say, while receiving a very hearty up and down hand shaking. "I'm Charity."

"Oh, we all know that," says a voice coming into the kitchen. I turn around to see someone who is obviously Luke's brother; they could almost be twins but not quite. Luke's muscled body is much broader than his brother's for a start. Besides that, the lookalike is slightly shorter and wears his hair practically shaven off, making him almost bald.

"I'm Pete, and I'm delighted to meet you after all these years."

"Hi," is all I can manage. *Years?*

"Moving on," says Luke, putting his arm around my shoulder and drawing me into the living room. "This is Lisa, and the two mischief-makers on the floor are my nieces Poppy and Rose."

"Hi," I wave at them. "Nice to meet you, and wow what pretty names you girls have."

"Thanks," they call back in unison without lifting their heads away from their dolls.

By the time an hour has passed I'm laughing my head off and totally at home. The banter between Shirley and Dave is very sweet, and it's wonderful to see that some people, even after forty years of marriage, can still be head-over-heels in love. There's a lot of camaraderie and back slapping between Luke and Pete, and the girls are complete chatter boxes. The only one that's slightly more reserved is Lisa, but she's charming and warm and I think she's just happy letting the rest of them get on with it.

Dinner is wonderful. Luke certainly hadn't exaggerated when he'd told me his mum was a great cook. It was one of the best roast dinners I've ever eaten.

101

After a few board games in the living room after dinner, Lisa offers to wash up and I jump up to help her.

"How long have you been married?" I ask.

"Nine years now. Although, I have no idea where the time has gone."

"You must have been young when you got married."

"Twenty-one. At the time I felt very grown up, now I know I was still a babe. I think in hindsight I would have waited a few years before getting married, but we're here now. Most importantly we're happy and healthy. So tell me… is it serious between you two?"

I freeze slightly at the abrupt question. "We've only just started dating," is the only thing I can think of to answer.

"And your husband's not been dead long either."

Ouch, that felt like a slap. I carry on drying a plate. What do I say? "That's right, he only died just over four months ago."

"Don't you think it's too soon to start dating?"

Well, yes I do actually. And I've been having that internal dialogue with myself continually, but I'll be blowed if I'll let someone else put me down. "Roland and I had been living separate lives for a few years, so I think that eased the sorrow of his passing."

There must have been something in the tone of my voice, because Lisa takes her gloves off and wraps her arms around me. "I'm sorry," she says stepping away again. She wraps her arms around herself and looks at me as if gauging what to say.

"When Tanya died, Luke was beside himself. He couldn't get out of bed for months, we really feared for him. It took him a long time to recover."

"He's told me she was a wonderful person who enjoyed life."

"She was very outgoing and very outspoken too. Often rubbed people up the wrong way, but Luke would never have a word said against her. He's a true Scorpio you know. He's a volcano of emotions held tightly together under that skin of his. He's serious and reliable, trustworthy and caring. He's also not had another girlfriend since Tanya died."

"Oh." Now I can see what the third degree has been all about. Was I serious? Was I going to hurt him? "We've only just started dating, but I can tell you I think very highly of him."

"He's been in love with you for years you know."

"What?"

"Agh, sorry you didn't know. He'd been quiet for so many years, just getting on with his job and not really going out, despite Pete's efforts to get him dating again. Then one day he came home and told us he'd just driven home the most beautiful woman he'd ever seen. That was you."

I can't reply, I'm too stunned and overwhelmed.

"Over the last three years he's done nothing but talk about you."

"Oh blimey, good things I hope."

Lisa laughed. "Nothing but good things."

I'm trying to work out in my head what on earth he could have said about me. I shake my head. I just can't picture a conversation about me.

"Hey pet, the girls are getting restless. You nearly done in here?" Pete asks from the doorway. I wonder how long he's been there.

"You go," I say. "I'm happy to finish off, there's not much left."

"You sure?"

"Yep." I pick up the rubber gloves and get straight into the sink. I can hear them getting ready to leave after a while.

"Bye," they all call from the doorway.

"Bye," I call back, "lovely to meet you."

I hear the parents waving them off on the drive as I continue with the last of the dishes.

"Hello you." Luke snakes his arms around my waist and kisses my shoulder.

"Hey you." It feels so natural that I'm not even embarrassed when Shirley comes in the kitchen.

She gently nudges me away from the sink. "We'll finish them later. Come and watch the news with us. Boris is about to make an announcement."

My heart drops. For a few hours, I'd been caught up in the happiness that is family life and had firmly pushed Coronavirus out of my mind. Dave has already got the television on and we all sit down to watch. There is something very poignant about the moment and I wish Nana was here with us.

The news is disheartening. Figures are being reported on the youngest person known to have died of Coronavirus at just eighteen years old. Knowing he had underlying issues doesn't really take the sadness of it away. The Nursing and Midwifery Council announce more than 5,600 former employees have signed up to return to work. The sheer weight of the situation sits on me like an elephant and I can't help crying. Luke moves closer and wraps his arms around me. Shirley takes a tissue from a box for herself and then passes it to me.

"Thanks," I croak.

The filming of certain television programs has now come to a halt. The cameras show you people still meeting in public. Finally, the voice of Boris floods the front room. *'We are all in this together. If we don't stay at home and protect the NHS they will be unable to cope. Non-essential travel has to stop. Tougher measures may be brought in. We are living in unprecedented times.'*

Suddenly, I'm flooded with guilt. I shouldn't be here. I shouldn't be away from home and I certainly shouldn't have left Nana on her own. "Time for me to go, I think," I say with a sniffle as I stand up.

Shirley jumps straight up and hugs me. "I'm not sure when this will be over, but I am very glad we managed to have today and get to know each other."

"Aww, thank you. I feel the same," I reply, hugging her tight. "Night," I wave to Dave, "please don't get up. Luke will see me out."

"You look after yourself, young lady."

I want to cry again as his parting comment is said with such sincerity.

Luke does up the buttons on my coat. "Will you be OK to drive home on your own?"

"Yes, I'll be fine."

"Call me as soon as you're there to let me know you're safe."

There's that warm sense of being loved and cared for again. I smile up at him, albeit with sad eyes. "Will do."

Once more, Luke wraps his huge hands around my cheeks and lifts my face towards him. "I know this is too soon for you, but I love you. With all that's going on in the world right now I just have to tell you. We don't know what tomorrow may bring, so I need to tell you now. I love you. I have loved you for a long time. I would never have wished anything bad to happen to Roland, and I'm sorry for his death which came too soon. But there is also a part of me that can't help being happy that you're here with me. I'm sorry if I'm burdening you, but I think I will explode if I don't tell you."

Pearls of water slide down my cheeks and Luke wipes them away with his thumbs. "I'm sorry, I knew it was too soon for you."

I stretch up on tiptoes, cup his face with my hands and bring him down towards me. Our kiss is long. Sentiment poured into an expression of longing and wanting. I think my answer is obvious, but I can't bring myself to actually say I love you, too.

Chapter 13

NANA AND I CLASP HANDS as we watch Boris Johnson's speech. It's Monday the 23rd March, and the UK is going into lockdown.

> 'This is the biggest threat this country has ever seen. If we don't act now, this invisible killer will have a devastating impact on our National Health Service. Without a huge national effort to halt the spread of the growth of this virus, there will come a moment when no health service in the world could possibly cope. Our efforts are vital to slow the spread of disease so we can protect the NHS's ability to cope and save more lives. You **must** stay at home. Shopping should only be for necessities; one amount of outdoor exercise can be done each day; any medical need for traveling is allowed, as is work only for those who are unable to work from home. No prime minister wants to enact measures like this. But remember, we are in this together.'

His six-minute speech is over. Life as we know it has just changed. We are most definitely living in unprecedented times. The enormity of the situation weighs heavy in the air. The clock on the mantel ticks with the rising crescendo in a horror film. The world is under attack, and it's not a nuclear bomb as predicted by Nostradamus, it's a virus that has apparently sprung out of China. It might as well be a weapon of mass destruction for the amount of fear it has created. The unknown - the biggest fear of all. Will this be like the Spanish Flu, where a quarter of the population in the United Kingdom was affected? Please God, no.

"I think I'll just go and check that Cathy is alright," says Nana standing up.

"Nana, you can't go out. You've just this second heard we have to stay indoors."

"Yes, but it's just next door. I'll just check they have everything they need. They're getting on a bit now you know."

"Nana, they're younger than you! If you really want to check on them we can give them a call."

Dotty stands still looking at me with a blank expression.

"Are you OK, Nana?" I reach out and put my arm around her waist. "Come on into the kitchen. I'll pop the kettle on. We'll have a nice cup of tea and then you can ring if you like."

"You know I've had a pneumonia vaccination, I'm absolutely sure this flu won't affect me."

"That was twenty-eight years ago, Nana. I hardly think it's still working in you today." I fill the kettle and switch it on. Dotty reaches for the cups.

"I nearly died of pneumonia when I was a young girl, that's why they gave me the vaccine. I was lucky to receive it."

"Yes, you were. But you're not to go thinking you're immune to this Coronavirus, do you hear me?"

"Loud and clear. Anyone would think I was deaf!"

"Nana, this is serious. Please, I couldn't bear it if anything happened to you." My throat catches and I'm crying, yet again. I have absolutely no idea where all the salty water comes from.

"Aww, my little love, we'll be fine you'll see. It will all blow over in a couple of months and we'll get back to normal before you know it."

"You have to promise me you won't go out. You heard what they said, the over eighty-fives are at high risk, Nana please."

"Sweetheart," Dotty takes my hands in hers and strokes them. "You must remember that I'm not going home to Heaven a day before I'm supposed to. The Lord will bring me home when He's good and ready and not a day before. If anything were to happen to me, you need to remember that. You promise *me* that you'll also remember that leaving this world is not the end of life. It is the beginning, and praise God we'll meet again in paradise, trust me."

For the first time in my life I wish I had Nana's faith. "I promise to remember what you've said," I say, gathering her in for a hug.

The extent to which we are blessed has been impacting me more and more over these first two weeks of lockdown. I can't imagine how terrible it must be for families with young children to be cooped up in a flat. Sunshine pours down on us like an eternal blessing, like a promise of hope and the comfort of a warm blanket. If only it would bring a cure.

We've been in the garden most days pottering around. Weeding and trimming mostly, and planting a huge number of incredibly cheap geraniums that I found in the supermarket. In the afternoon when Dotty takes a nap on the sofa, I have been lying back on the sun-lounger and reading. I've got to admit I feel like I'm on holiday. Life is slow, leisurely and brimming over with people wanting to spread goodwill. There are moments in humanity that bring me to tears with the overwhelming intentions of people 'doing their bit.'

As the death toll rises, we find ourselves glued to the evening news watching the graphs and listening intently to everything. We feel cocooned in our comfortable home, removed from the horrors going on in other people's lives and within the hospitals. Still, the pair of us cry every day, at each sad story that appears. How blessed are we, so totally blessed. So blessed in fact, that I've started praying! I know, it was a shock to me too when I first realized what I was doing. I started with the Lord's Prayer, but slowly over the weeks I've started beseeching Him with requests for all these sick people, and those who look after them. I guess He must be inundated at that moment. He probably doesn't consider mine to be high on His priority list; still there is a need in me to reach out to Him. My church upbringing pours back to me with the ease of slipping into a warm, soapy bath. It's strange because a part of me has the sense that I've never been away. I might not have been praying or attending church, but somehow God has always been here. It's a weird understanding, yet one that brings me much comfort.

Despite lockdown the purchase of the company went ahead and my bank account has been topped up. The purchase of the cottages in Wales has also gone ahead. When this virus has run its course, we will have a meeting and set the date for the first youth venture week.

Zoom has turned into a marvelous tool, and I've spoken to both solicitors and Megan using it. It has also kept me close to Luke. We might not be able to be together, but talking every day on Zoom is a pretty close second to actually being with one another.

It's Tuesday April 7th. I've been up since five. Something restless in my spirit has called me to make a cup of tea and to sit in the kitchen with Nana's Bible. I've been praying against the virus and asking for help for everyone working in hospitals. On last night's news report we had watched pizzas being delivered to hospital staff. They're struggling under the volume of people coming in with Covid19. The camera had moved over nurses sleeping on the floor and the grief I feel for all involved is overwhelming. Please, God we need your help.

THUD! I shudder at the sudden noise. Then I jump to my feet, waiting. Nothing follows. I rush out of the kitchen and up the stairs.

"Nana, Nana. Are you OK?"

Silence is the foreboding of ill tidings. Silence, where Nana's voice should be. I charge into her room. She's lying on the floor. The scream that comes from me is unearthly. Dropping to the floor I touch her face.

"Nana, Nana." She moans and I nearly throw up with relief. "What happened? Nana, can you hear me?" I stroke her hair off her face. "Nana?"

She moans again, trying to talk to me. She lifts one arm. I'm not a doctor or a nurse but I take a quick guess that she's just had a stroke. I pull the pillow off her bed and tenderly lift her head to put it under her.

"I'm calling an ambulance, Nana. I'll be right back."

She mumbles something incomprehensible.

I rush downstairs, grab the landline and dial 999. Please, God, I know they're busy with the virus, but Please, God, please let there be an ambulance close by.

"999. Fire, police or ambulance?"

I explain to the operator what has happened, and she asks me to stay on the phone.

"I can't," I yell, trying very hard to stay calm. "I've got to go back up to her." The operator is an angel. She talks until I'm calm. Then she tells me to unlock the front door for the paramedics who will be here soon. She asks me for my cell number and tells me I can put the phone down and she'll call me back on the cell so I can go back upstairs.

Thank God for the NHS. Where would we be without all your marvelous staff? I have no idea how long it took, but suddenly, someone is calling 'hello' in the doorway.

"Up here," I call back.

As they come through the bedroom door covered in their PPE I realize they're about to take Dotty to a place where she

112

might catch the virus. Sudden panic grips me and I start sobbing.

A female paramedic puts her arms around me. "We'll take good care of her."

"Can I come with you?"

"I'm sorry, you can't. As soon as she is settled in hospital someone will call you, but I'm afraid I can't tell you how long that will take."

The other two paramedics have finished checking Dotty over and have put her onto a stretcher. She's moaning, which causes me to sob some more. I walk downstairs with them and stand on the drive as they move away.

"God you have to make her well, Please, God I couldn't stand it if she left me as well."

"What's happened?"

I look up to see Cathy and Mike in their pajamas over the waist high hedge between our drives.

"I don't know, but I think she may have had a stroke."

"Oh God! How dreadful. Oh, we're so sorry, love. I wish I could come over there and give you a hug," says Cathy.

"So do I," I answer. "Excuse me, but I think I need to sit down."

"OK, dear, but please call us if there is anything we can do," replies Cathy.

"I will do." After I close the front door I have no energy to go anywhere and simply slide down the door. "Oh, please God, please God," is all I can say.

I'm not sure how long I've been on the floor, but suddenly my cell is ringing and I realize I've left it upstairs. I charge up the stairs, panicking now that the hospital is calling me already with bad news. As I reach for it I can see Luke's name.

"Luke," I wail down the phone.

"What is it? What's happened?"

I tell him in between sobs.

"I'll be with you in an hour." With that Luke hangs up, leaving me staring at the blank screen. We're not allowed to mix households, what's he going to do, offer to comfort me through the front room window? It won't help. The moment I see him I am going to want to be in his arms.

I know Nana likes to keep a tidy house, so after leaving the door on the latch for Luke, to keep busy I make her bed and open the curtains to let some light in. I trace my hand along the multi-colored quilt. Nana had it for as long as I can remember. She'd made it years ago when she was part of the church sewing group. I remember the years that she sat sewing night after night, making up quilts to send to orphanages in places like Romania. She was always busy and involved in different missions and fund-raisers.

She's lived a good life. At first the thought is comforting, assurance that Nana has filled her life with love and good deeds. The next moment I'm drowning in the fact that it refers to the possibility her life might be over. I drop onto her bed. Pulling a pillow out from under the quilt I bury my face in it, breathing in the slight aroma of Nana's lavender perfume. Sobs wrack through me, tears soak the pillow.

"Charity?" The yell from downstairs jerks me out of my heavy-eyed doze.

"Luke." I'm off the bed and running towards the stairs. Luke is already half-way up them, taking them two at a time. I wait for him.

"Oh, babes. I'm sorry, how is she? Have you heard from the hospital?"

I shake my head, I can't talk.

Luke engulfs me in his arms, pressing my head against his chest with his hand. The oaky-musky smell of his aftershave wafts over me. The warmth of his body sooths me. I melt, like butter on hot toast.

"You shouldn't be here," I whisper.

"I've brought my stuff with me. I'm staying until Dotty comes home."

I'm too relieved to say anything. Right now I don't ever want him to leave, not even when Nana comes home. We might have only been dating for months, but I already know I want to spend the rest of my life with him. If nothing else, then this virus has shown me that life is too short. We never know which day will be our last, and I don't want to waste any of those that I have left.

I wait three hours before I can stand it no longer and call the hospital. The phone rings and rings with no answer. On my third call someone picks up. Abruptly I'm told that the doctor will ring me when he's able. It does nothing to calm my stress. I try to rationalize how busy they must be, and how many patients they must have to see. But Nana is my only concern right now and the waiting is downright awful.

At 1 pm Luke makes us some sandwiches and a pot of tea. I try, but I just can't eat. At 1.20 pm my cell rings. It is a number I don't recognize.

"Hello?"

"Mrs. Byron?"

"Yes, that's me."

"This is Doctor Kennington, calling from Macclesfield Hospital."

There is something about his official, serious tone that warns me. "Is she alright?"

"Mrs. Byron, can you confirm that you are the next of kin to Mrs. Dorothy Williams?"

"Ooh," I have no control of the wail of pain that escapes me.

"Mrs. Byron, do you have someone with you?"

Luke guides me to the chair and sits me down, before gently prising the cell out of my hand.

"Hello, I am a friend of the family. Mrs. Byron is struggling to talk right now. Can you give me the update please?"

I hear a muffled question coming from the phone as I rock back and forth.

"Luke Smith, close friend to both Mrs. Williams and her granddaughter Mrs. Byron, who is with me now."

More muffled conversation.

"I understand. Can you explain what happens now please?"

Endless talk which I blank out. I don't want to know. I don't want to know. I don't want to know.

Luke has shifted and is kneeling in front of me.

"Babe…"

"Oh no, nooooo, don't say it!"

"I'm sorry, babe. Apparently, she was unconscious by the time they arrived at hospital. She died two hours ago. They have to complete some tests for the death certificate, but they feel confident that she suffered from a massive stroke."

I want to die. I want to curl up and die. "Aaah" I can't help the wailing, it flows from my stomach and out of me in a release of acute pain. Luke picks me up and sits down, cradling me on his lap. As much as I can, I am curled into a ball like a child. Luke rocks me, hushing me and stroking my hair. I don't know how long we sit there.

Chapter 14

ONLY IMMEDIATE FAMILY ARE ALLOWED to attend Dotty's funeral. I lied. I don't care. I told the vicar taking the service at the graveside that Luke's my fiancé. I couldn't have done it without him. You see, all there is left of Dotty's family is me. She was an only child, my mum was Dotty's only child, and I am my mum's only daughter. I am the end of the line for us. If I don't have children, our family tree will come to an end.

Loads of people came and lined the pavement to the church. All at a safe distance from each other, obeying the guidelines but paying their respects to a beloved member of their church family. I'm moved so much as they nod at me, offer a word of comfort and a promise to celebrate Dotty's life when we go back to normal. Lord above, will we ever go back to normal?

I'm struggling so much with the fact that Nana attended church her entire life, but at her death is denied a service in church. It's not right. It's not fair. How can a handful of people around a hole in the ground do tribute to the life of a wonderful woman? I feel like she's been robbed. It's salt being rubbed into a wound that is already raw. Not only is the service outdoors, but regretfully the vicar has two ceremonies to perform after Nana's so I feel like we're on a conveyor belt. It's all so wrong, understandable with the current state of affairs, but still painful.

It's our first argument. OK, maybe it's just the first clash of wills. It's not like we're shouting or anything.

"I'll be fine here. It's OK, you go home. Your mum needs you."

"And how am I supposed to look after my mum, when all I will be doing is worrying about you? Stop being so stubborn and just come with me."

This conversation had been going back and forth for the last hour, ever since Luke's brother had called to say their dad was suspected of having Coronavirus and the ambulance had just taken him to Stepping Hill Hospital.

"I can't just impose myself upon your mum. She has enough to worry about."

"Instead of considering yourself a hindrance, why don't you think that you might actually be able to help *her*?"

Ouch, that bucket of cold water jolted. Was I really only thinking of myself by refusing to go?

"I suppose I could help with the cooking and everything. She probably won't feel like cooking or cleaning until... until he comes home." Please, God, he *will* come home.

"Great, that's settled then. I'll go around the house making sure everything is locked up and appliances switched off. You go and throw a few things together."

I run up the stairs. It's true the last few days since Dotty's funeral have been nothing more than wallowing in my grief, I figured I'm allowed. I'd lost my husband and my only relative (I don't even think about dad anymore) and isn't grief better out than in? Sure I read that somewhere. I grab a small hold-all and start throwing things in. Toiletries, pajamas, another pair of jeans and a few tops. That will do.

Obviously, we are about to break the rules once again. But we're not hopping back and forth, we're going to go and stay and become one unit. It's bad enough that Shirley can't go to hospital with Dave. At least we can be there to support her. Both Luke and I are young and healthy. I've also been plying us with hearty multi-vitamins and immunity-building foods. I'm confident we won't catch it. Still, a part of me is wondering if the police will stop our car on the way and ask us where we're going.

"Ready," I announce as I come bounding down the stairs. Luke looks up, and his white face and black-ringed eyes suddenly strike me. Oh, sweet man, how hard this must be for you, you're such a close family.

I drop my bag by his feet and lift my arms to wrap around his neck. He bends down a little so I can reach. "I'm sorry Luke, I'm sure your dad will be OK, he's a fighter isn't he?"

He pushes his face into my hair and just stands still for a moment. Eventually, pulling up he takes a deep breath and straightens up. "Come on, let's go."

The roads are incredibly empty. There's a part of me that wishes they were like this all the time. I've loved the silence the lockdown has created. The chirping of the birds now seems so loud. The glorious sunshine encourages our feathered friends in joyous song. A modicum of restoration giving the world a much needed re-boot. A moment in time to repair the ozone layer and de-pollute the air we breathe. Minus the virus and the economy crashing it would be amazing to carry on this way. What a shame that everything will return to normal. Will we go back to normal? Absorbed in my contemplative narrative, as we pull onto his parents' driveway I'm surprised that we've got here so quickly.

The door opens before we reach it. Shirley is a mess and has obviously been crying for hours. I'm flooded with remorse for not coming sooner. It's obvious that she's about to launch herself into Luke's arms. He takes a step back and puts out his arm to stop her.

"Mum, let us go in first and wash. We'll scrub from top to bottom to make sure we're not bringing germs in."

I can't help thinking that maybe, as this is the house that might have Coronavirus in it, that the scrubbing should be the other way round. As if reading my thoughts, Shirley declares,

"I've been scrubbing all day. You could eat your dinner off that floor. As for my hands they're raw from all the washes. I boil washed all our clothes, and I've been extra vigilant with everything from the moment your dad felt unwell. I'm positive you won't catch anything." She is pleading. Her whole demeanor is screaming to be hugged.

Luke takes a step forward and engulfs his mum in a massive hug. She is crying instantly. I take the bags from the boot of the car.

"Come on, Mum. Let's get inside."

"I've made homemade lemonade," Shirley sniffles. "It's supposed to be good for fighting off colds. Fetch it from the fridge Luke, and bring it into the garden. It's cool on the patio."

"I'll fetch it," I say, giving Shirley a gentle smile.

"Oh, love," she says throwing herself at me. "I'm so sorry about your Nan." Her arms hold me in a vice as she urges her compassion to be conveyed.

"Thank you," I say into her mop of curly blonde hair. When she lets me go, I smile at Luke and head into the

121

kitchen. It doesn't take long to put the jug and glasses on a tray and bring them into the garden. Shirley's right about the temperature. The pergola that covers the patio is smothered in yellow flowered honeysuckle, and deep burnt-orange clematis. The thick green canopy throws the patio into shade, while the welcome, soporific breeze offers a token of coolness.

"So tell us what happened exactly," says Luke, taking a sip of his lemonade.

"On Monday he woke up complaining he was out of sorts. He said he felt like he had a cold coming on and moved out of our room and slept in the spare room so as not to pass it to me. Yesterday, this racking cough came out of nowhere. I called the doctor straight away, but she said it was too early to tell if it was Coronavirus or just a common cold. She told me to ring for an ambulance if he got worse. He struggled to eat some soup; every time he tried he just kept coughing. I gave him some soluble multivitamins to help build him up, and he did seem to perk up a little in the evening." Shirley pauses to take a drink.

"Then this morning he didn't want to get out of bed and he wouldn't let me come in the bedroom. He shouted at me when I tried to come in, and that set him off coughing again. I called for an ambulance straight away. I didn't take his temperature but I could see from the doorway that he was boiling hot. He was sweating something terrible." Shirley is choking up and starts crying. I automatically lean over and wrap my arms around her.

"Fetch us a tissue, love," she says to Luke.

"I'll get it," I say about to stand up.

"Hush you, stay there. Luke will go."

Shirley takes my hands in hers, and takes a deep breath. "I've made up both the spare bedrooms. Will you be needing one or two rooms?"

I can feel the heat rushing up from my neck to my cheeks. "It would be nice to have my own room please. But I'm sorry you've had to go to that trouble."

She gives my hand a little squeeze. "No trouble at all. It is lovely to have you here, and I mean that."

I've got a small lump in my throat. "Thank you," I croak.

"Here we go," says Luke putting the box of tissues on the table. "So what happens now, Mum?"

"Now we wait and get down on our knees and pray."

The only update we receive by the end of the day is that he's comfortable. It's very hard to watch the news that night, yet we are, it seems, addicted to the daily updates. We're ever watchful for the turn of events to worsen, morbid yet somehow obsessive.

I do a double-take at the clock. It's 9.30! I jump out of bed in a flurry. How could I have slept so long? I went to bed at ten, it's not like I was up late. I grab my clothes and rush to the bathroom for a quick shower. I can hear Luke and his mum downstairs talking. I don't know what they're saying but a sense of family comes over me, it's warm and cozy.

"Good morning, sleepy-head," says Luke giving me a kiss on the forehead. "No need to ask if you slept well, we heard you did!" He chortles as he sees the look on my face, which must be reflecting the horror I'm experiencing.

"I didn't snore, did I?"

"Rafters were shaking," Luke nearly bends double laughing so much.

"It wasn't that bad, dear," says Shirley coming over and patting my shoulder. "Come and sit down. Would you like some tea or coffee?"

"Coffee please, but I can make it."

"Don't be daft. Sit down. I've got to keep busy or I'll go crazy."

Luke, who has suddenly returned to very serious, and I exchange glances behind Shirley's back. "Any news?" I say softly.

Luke shakes his head.

"We'll find out more when I call shortly," says Shirley.

We can't get Shirley to sit down after that. From making the coffee she moves on to washing a few dishes in the sink. Eventually, it is time to call. We gather in the front room and Luke dials and puts the phone on loudspeaker. The phone is answered immediately by Mary, one of the nurses on the ward.

"Mrs. Smith, your husband would like to say hello to you. Do you have Zoom at all, or FaceTime?"

"I have both on my iPad," I volunteer.

"Great," replies the nurse. "I'll give you my details, if you call me straight away before I get busy again, I can take you to see Mr. Smith."

There's two minutes of flurrying around as I grab a piece of paper and a pen to write down her details. We call her back straight away.

The screen shows 'calling' only for a moment and then flickers and there is Dave on the screen. He is rested back against pillows, there's an oxygen mask lying on his chest but not over his mouth.

"MORNING LOVE," Shirley shouts.

"Not deaf yet, you old bat," says Dave before having a coughing fit.

"Oh, that's so clear," says Shirley looking at Luke and I in surprise.

"Modern technology is wonderful," I answer.

We only get to talk for five minutes before the nurse apologizes and explains she needs to get on. She promises to call us back in the evening if she can.

"You've been given the name Mary for a reason. You're a saint, can't tell you how much this means to me," says Shirley breaking down into tears.

"You're welcome. I can't promise to call you back, but I will if I can."

In the evening Shirley speaks with a doctor at the hospital. Dave has unfortunately caught Coronavirus, but he's comfortable and they are doing all they can for him. After the call, Shirley cries for about half an hour before admitting to being exhausted and going to bed. I go into the kitchen to wash the evening meal dishes. After about five minutes I hear Luke climb the stairs. I can hear them talking, something in me stills and I stop the washing up. I'm curious so I go to stand at the bottom of the stairs. Luke is praying with his mum. I'm overwhelmed with the beauty of such an act. A little thing maybe, but it must be such a comfort to Shirley. What a wonderful man! And to think he drove me around for years and I hardly noticed him. Life is strange.

I've just finished the last of the dishes when Luke comes in. There is so much going on right now in the world, life seems crazy. Losing Nana has been terrible. Dave going into hospital is frightening. And yet I look at this tall handsome man and my heart melts. There are good things in the world, and he is one of them.

We hug for a while, gently swaying, peaceful and loving. "Come on, let's watch something and try to switch off for a while."

"Good idea," Luke answers.

We cuddle on the sofa. We're so relaxed together now it's like we're an old married couple. My head lies against his chest, I sigh softly. I could stay here forever.

The waiting game is painful. Minutes roll into hours and hours into days, and all the time we are on tenterhooks. Shirley is losing weight. I've tried cooking tempting meals, but nothing is more appealing than two or three mouthfuls. Luke is beside himself. His boss is telling him if he doesn't come back to work soon he's going to lose his job. When most of Britain has gone onto furlough it just doesn't seem fair. In the end he's given holiday, but has to go in tomorrow for an important job. Really he's a chauffeur, what could be so important that only he could do the driving? Luke has to explain that some of his customers trust him more than others, so when they're off somewhere they don't want the press or prying eyes to look they ask for him.

"I've made ginger and butternut squash soup," I announce, standing in the doorway.

"I don't fancy anything to eat, thank you though," says Shirley.

"Mum, you've got to eat! You're worrying me to bits. Please just come and try a little, Charity's been in the kitchen for hours."

Yikes, no emotional pressure there then! It works though, and Shirley comes into the kitchen with Luke. I've cooked some part-baked bread and the smell is delicious mixed with the aroma from the soup. I'm keeping my fingers crossed we can tempt her.

"This is fab," says Luke after his third spoonful.

"Thanks," I smile back.

Shirley doesn't say anything but by the time she's put the fifth spoonful in her mouth I sigh with relief. I've made something to entice her at last. She manages to eat half the bowl, and I'm pleased as punch.

Out of the blue Shirley says. "You must miss your Nan so much."

I had a spoon half-way up to my mouth; I put it down in the bowl without eating. "I do."

"How do you get through the day?"

I know why she's asked. She's trying to imagine how she could possibly cope if Dave doesn't come home. I wipe my mouth with a napkin.

"Not long before Nana died, she told me that she wouldn't die until God was ready to take her home. She also told me that we'll meet again in Paradise." I stumble over the last words. They still evoke waterfalls of emotions within me.

"That's true, but I don't think I would want to wait. I think I would want to go to Heaven straight away."

"Mum! You can't say that! What about us? What about Poppy and Rose? What would we do if you both went at the

127

same time? It would be too much. You can't think like that."

I reach under the table and grab his hand, squeezing it tight.

"I'm just thinking out loud. I don't mean I will top myself or anything. Heaven forbid. It's just I can't imagine…" She bursts into tears and both of us jump up at the same time to hug her.

As if God is watching… my iPad starts ringing. We all jump up and run into the front room where I've left it on the coffee table. I swipe the answer button and Nurse Mary's smiling face appears. Gosh but she looks like an angel.

"I've got someone here who wants to say hello," she grins.

Dave has been in hospital for six days now. For the last few days he's been on a ventilator to help him breath. As Mary turns her phone around so we can see Dave we hold our breath. The ventilator has gone and Mary has propped him up.

Dave gives us a flicker of a smile. "How's my sweet girl doing?"

Mary is laughing and crying at the same time. "I'm doing fine, love. How about you, how are you today?"

Luke and I sit back and let Shirley talk to Dave. He's looking quite gaunt and his cheeks are still flushed, but his eyes seem to be so much clearer. He coughs in-between short sentences, his voice is weak and faltering, but for all that there's joy because he's not on the ventilator anymore!

"I'm not going to let this bugger kill me off, Shirley. Got years left in me yet. I'll be home before you know it. You keep that bed warm for me."

"I will love, oh I will."

After five minutes he's obviously tiring and Mary tells them to say goodnight.

That night as I clasp my hands in prayer my heart overflows with gratitude, for not everyone who catches Coronavirus dies.

Chapter 15

"YOU'VE GOT TO SEE THIS!" I've watched it three times already, boy it brings such joy I can't stop smiling and I want to dance!

"What is it?" asks Luke coming over. I pass him my iPad and press play again, turning the volume up. Michael and Ali Hoffman are lip-syncing to Jess Glynne's 'Hold my Hand' and dancing around their kitchen. It's such fun! They've done it as part of Quarantine Challenge 2K20.

"Oh, that's brill," says Luke.

"What are you listening to?" asks Shirley.

"Come and see," I say passing it to her.

Within ten seconds, Shirley is bouncing her head and shaking her hips.

"Go disco diva," laughs Luke breaking into dance himself.

Well I can't let them dance alone, can I? I'm straight into rocking, shoulders, hips and arms wobbling all over the place. We're all bouncing up and down. Feel good music, wow what an amazing thing it is. When we've danced to it no less than three times we decide to put YouTube on the television and see what else we can find to dance to.

Two hours later we are totally exhausted and thoroughly relaxed. Half way through, we Zoom-called Pete, and then Lisa, Poppy and Rose had all joined in dancing with us in their own front room. We'd had such a good time. It was a shame we couldn't actually be together but we did have an amazing time. I guess if lockdown hadn't happened I never

130

would have been here, and I wouldn't be dancing with them and experiencing such a sense of belonging. It's the little things isn't it? It didn't cost any money but I've had a better time here than I'd had at my party that cost so much money I can't stand to think of it anymore.

"It's almost time," announces Shirley. We get up and join her in the hallway, then the three of us step outside onto the driveway and walk down to the pavement. It's Thursday, it's 8 pm and it's time to clap. We not only clap for all we're worth, we whoop and cheer in between calling out to say hi to the neighbors. We would be here anyway, but maybe today our hearts are brimming over with gratitude just a little more than normal for the NHS, for tomorrow Dave will be coming home.

"Whoop, whoop," I yell. I would clap by a microphone if I could to make it louder. Blooming marvelous people. Working and dying trying to save people they don't know. I take my hat off to them, there are no words to describe our gratitude, I guess that's why we're clapping. The idea might have sprung out of the Netherlands and been instigated in London by a Dutch expatriate called Annemarie Plas, but boy were we making it our own now. The clapping in our street lasts nearly ten minutes. The kids in the house next door are banging pots and shaking maracas and absolutely enjoying being allowed to make so much noise.

"How's Dave doing?" a neighbor from across the street calls once the clapping has stopped.

"Marvelous! He's coming home tomorrow, praise God," answers Shirley.

"Oh, praise God," the neighbor calls back.

131

"That's great news," calls another person higher up the street.

We wave at everyone and go back inside. It has been simply the best of days.

Its four o'clock before Dave finally arrives home. Luke had persuaded his mum to let him pick his Dad up, and Shirley had been pacing the house most of the day. She rushes to the car the moment the engine switches off. The door flies open and Dave and Shirley sob on each other. My waterworks are flowing, it's just too touching.

"Come on, Mum, out the way, let me get Dad in." Shirley reluctantly steps back and Luke helps his dad get out of the car. He's lost so much weight he looks like half the man he once was. He manages a smile though as they go past me, and I can see a twinkle in his eye. He can only walk a few steps on his own. He's gasping for breath by the time Luke gets him into the tall backed chair in the front room.

"Are you sure you don't want to go to bed, Dad?"

"Not on your life, son. I want to sit here and look at you all, all day long!"

"The doctors said you are still in for a hard time and you've got to look after yourself. Recovery can be slow," chastens Luke.

Shirley pulls a chair up next to Dave, and taking his hand in hers she brings it up to her lips to kiss him. "God is good," she says softly.

"He is indeed," answers Dave with a sigh.

I want that. That love which is pure and true and survives the test of time. The love that is selfless. That love that means there will never be another for you for as long as you live. The love where marriage vows are honored and true. No cheating. No ignoring. No disrespecting. Just caring, tender and honest. I turn around quickly, and go into the kitchen to start on the dinner. I can't believe the emotions that have fought for pole-position in my mind these last six months. So much has changed. Yet... I don't want to go back.

"What do you want me to do?" asks Luke.

"Peel some spuds if you like. I'm making cottage pie for tea. It's soft and hopefully your dad will be able to swallow it ok."

Luke comes up behind and puts his arms around my waist. He nuzzles into my neck and whispers. "I love you."

I love you too, but I'm too choked up right now to tell you.

After dinner we gather to watch the daily updates. Boris announces that Britain has passed the peak. He warns we mustn't risk a second spike and confirms he will be setting out a comprehensive plan for easing out of lockdown next week. 26,771 people have died so far due to Coronavirus in the UK. I can't help looking at Dave and thanking God in my head once more, that Dave is not one of them.

Next to come on the news is the celebration of Captain Tom Moore's 100th birthday! What an encouraging man, what a blooming marvelous attitude to have. I take my hat off to him. He is the embodiment of all that is British and personifies our stiff upper lip mentality. Starting off on April 6th he had set himself a goal to walk for donations for the NHS. His aim was to raise one thousand pounds before his birthday. He has done that today, but the amount he has raised by walking around his house on his Zimmer-frame is thirty-two million! It takes my breath away, not only his resolve to walk every day but the generosity of the British folk, especially as we're going through difficult times.

"Have you given anything yet, Shirley?" asks Dave, whose eyes are brimming over with tears.

"Yes love. I donated a hundred."

"Good stuff," he says blowing his nose.

The next couple of days are spent taking care of Dave and playing cards on the patio when he was sleeping. The days are sleepy and long. Although I feel welcome here, I'm beginning to miss my own space. I guess I'm getting a bit stir-crazy. I'm glad things are beginning to ease off; if I go home Luke and I can still be a bubble. Although, Pete wants to make his household a bubble with his mum and dad's, which I understand, so I'm not sure how it will work, but I think it's time for me to go home.

The next morning Luke and I go for our daily exercise, a long walk. Along the way I build up the courage and finally blurt out. "I think I'm going to go home tomorrow."

"OK."

Oh, well that went more easily than planned. Wait… does that mean he's ready for me to go home, does he want me to go? I take a deep breath and turn my face towards him.

Before I can say anything, Luke adds. "I've felt you distancing yourself for a little while now. I knew you would go home as soon as lockdown eased."

"It's not because I don't like being here, I do, I really do. I love your family. Everyone has been very welcoming to me since the first time I came over for Sunday dinner."

"It's good to know you love *someone*."

"What? What does that mean?"

"Nothing, forget it."

"You don't think I'm a loving person?" Boy that hurts.

"It's not that. Drop it. Anyway, I've got to go back to work full time now, so I'd pretty much be better off at home so that I can sleep during the day."

"Oh, you're leaving too?"

"Yes, I need to get some overtime in when I can; my bills have been piling up with all this time off work."

"You haven't been paid? That's terrible!"

"I've been paid, but I normally make nearly the same amount in tips as I do in my wages, so my income has dropped significantly. I've still got a mortgage to pay... Oh, I don't want to talk shop. All you need to know is that it's also a good time for me to go home, so the fact that you're ready to leave is just good timing."

Before, I was feeling caged up, now I'm like an abandoned waif. Just no pleasing some people!

We finish the walk in silence. With each step we take I feel a gap between us growing larger and larger. I feel like I've done something wrong, but I just don't know what it is.

"Luke!" shouts Dave. "You've got to come and see this; I've just been laughing for a full ten minutes."

"What is it?" asks Luke approaching him.

Dave can't move around much. We all help out trying to get him to walk a little further each day, but he's still exhausted after only a few short walks so he spends most of the time watching television or flicking through social media. "Look what I've found on Facebook." He passes his phone to Luke, who reads something and then bursts out laughing.

"That's a cracker, Dad."

"What's that?" I ask.

Luke hands the phone back to his dad without looking at me. Ouch, now he's slighting me, what on earth has got into him?

"Here you go, love. Have a gander at this joke."

Dave passes me his phone. I take a quick look and burst out laughing.

"Oh, that really is funny!"

"Some people have a wicked sense of humor don't they?" I say handing the phone back.

"You've got to laugh in life, Charity. If you can't see the funny side in most things, you're in for a pretty miserable ride."

"Talking of rides," says Luke, "just to let you know that both Charity and I will be going home today."

"What?" asks Shirley, rushing in from the hallway. "What's brought this on? Why are you both leaving? Has something happened?"

"No, Mum. I've got to get back to work and it will be easier for me to sleep at my place, and Charity has business things she needs to attend to."

"Oh! OK. So long as you're both alright. You know you're welcome to stay here as long as you like, don't you?" she says, looking straight at me.

"I do, and thank you. It's been a godsend being able to stay with you all. But I really do have things that need taking care of. Nana's hanging baskets are all going to be dead now for a start."

"Yes, I suppose life does go on, virus or not. Well, I will miss you dear, but you must know you're always welcome. You don't need an invite, just turn up whenever you want," replies Shirley.

"Thank you," I mumble, most humbly.

We're packed and ready to leave within half-an-hour. I hug Dave softly, so as not to crush his chest which is still causing him problems. Shirley is the same height as me. She regards me for a moment and I can see her chin wobbling as she holds back tears.

"You come back soon, you hear?"

I nod, and then we're hugging each other to death. I'm choked on emotions. I feel like I'm leaving my parents behind, a very large part of me doesn't want to go. But go I must. There is a time and a place for everything, and right now I belong at Nana's so I can sort her things and look after everything.

Luke drives me back. There's no conversation between us. I feel impoverished. Is this wonderful man slipping through my fingers? Am I really going to just let him go without a fight? He gets out of the car with me and hovers as I put the key in the door. When I open it I turn to him questioning, will he come in?

"I best get going."

That's a no then. Speak woman, speak! What on earth is wrong with you? Don't let him go like this.

"It's going to be strange being in a house on my own."

His blue eyes bore into me. Won't you kiss me? Please kiss me. Tell me everything's going to be OK.

"I'm working late tonight, not sure what time I will be up tomorrow, but I'll give you a quick call before I start the next shift and check you're OK."

I nod. "Thank you." Please kiss me.

Luke takes one last look at me and leaves. Just like that he's gone. What's happened? I just don't understand.

The house smells musty and it prompts me to move. I go around the rooms opening the windows to let fresh air in. Actually, I have tons to do. I need to do all the legal stuff, get bills changed to my name for a start. Dotty has left a will leaving the house and her small savings to me, so everything would be straight forward, but I still have to contact everyone.

I make a pot of coffee and then tackle the mountain of post piled up on the dining room table. First, I open them all with a miniature sword letter-opener, then open them all up and sort them into piles by priority.

Something is nagging at the back of my mind. I pause. What is it? I get up and wander around the house. At last, my eyes are drawn to a CD player in the kitchen. Nana used to love singing whilst she cooked. I unplug it and take it into the dining room and re-plug it in, then press play. Zach

Rolands starts singing Chain Breaker. I sit down listening to the words. Do I have chains? Can God remove my chains? Heat bursts inside me. My fingers start tingling. Is this you God? Are you here? You would think after all the crying I've done lately that I would have no tears left. Not true. They fall like a fast-flowing river, streaming down my cheeks unchecked. Is this you God? What are my chains?

An image of my dad springs before me. Dad? Then knowledge unfolds, you might say by itself, but I think God is leading the way. Unforgiveness lies within my soul like a black, oozing cancer. Entwined with this damning condemnation, towards my dad for abandoning me, is resentment and downright hate. What an ugly word, hate. A loathing, a detesting for the blood of my blood who cares not one iota for me. Who does that? Who gives life to a new creation and then abandons them to a cruel world? *Who does that?*

I'm a Survivor starts to float into the room, coming out of the player. I want to be a survivor, Lord. Show me please. How do I forgive? Help me? I don't know what else to do, so I fall to the floor and kneel. Clasping my hands in front of me, I cry out.

"God be with me, please. Show me the way. Help me to forgive my dad. Please show me the way so this insidious heartache may be removed from me. I don't want to live my life in the shadows anymore, fearing to love in case I am rejected. Oh, God, please show me the way."

After a while lost in prayer and sobs I feel prompted to switch the disc. I look through the shelves, and my fingers land on Lauren Daigle.

"OK, Lord." I replace the disc and press play. You Say escapes the speakers. Lauren's voice catches at something within me instantly. I feel a fluttering of wings within my chest. "Oh, Lord, oh Lord."

'You say I am loved when I can't feel a thing
You say I am strong when I think I am weak
You say I am held when I am falling short
When I don't belong, oh You say I am Yours'

The words of the song tear at my soul, ripping away years and years of rejection and beliefs of being worthless. The amazing realization that God has always been with me during my 'absence' and that He never once rejected me, crash into my soul like a gigantic wrecking ball. With a Berlin Wall impression, my barriers of self-preservation come crumbling down.

Chapter 16

LUKE'S NOT ANSWERING MY TEXTS. I've so much I want to say to him, have to say to him, but how can I do that if he won't talk to me? Three of my texts asked what I'd done wrong. I'm loath to call him in case he's driving a client, or I'm just chicken, I guess.

I'm so grateful that we're allowed to meet people out in public now. Judith has met me in the park and we're just about to go for a walk. It's so lovely to see her again.

"How have you been? Gosh, wish I could hug you. This is really hard isn't it?"

"You're telling me," answers Judith. "My parents have been in bits every time we've turned up in their garden to wave hello to them. Mum just won't stop crying. Sometimes I think we should stop going, it would be less painful."

"I know, must be so hard for them though, not being able to hug their grandchildren."

"I can't wait to go back to normal."

"Nor me," I answer. "How's John doing?" During the early stages of lockdown he'd been staying at a friend's house, who was also an ambulance driver, for fear of bringing Covid home to his kids.

"He's great. It was so hard with him staying away. He spoke to us every day through Zoom, but honestly it's not the same as having him home. The kids went mental when he turned up at the door and told them he'd come home."

"Must have been hard for you; having to do the home-schooling on your own."

"It isn't too bad actually. We've got books from the school to follow and we do a lot with help from the lessons they've put on-line. Technology is fantastic! I would have hated this years ago when we weren't all internet savvy! Also, thankfully, they've been able to play in the garden every day to burn off their energy. Thank God for this amazing weather."

"It really does feel like a godsend doesn't it."

"Sure does."

We exchange news for a while. I realize I've missed this one-on-one chatting a lot.

"So, Luke eh? Who'd have guessed?"

I grimace at her. "I wish it was me and Luke. Something's happened and he's not talking to me."

"Go and speak to him and get it sorted. It's probably something and nothing."

"He's not answering my texts."

"Charity! That's so impersonal. You need to go and see him, talk to him face to face, and just plain outright ask him what's wrong. You don't want to lose him do you?"

"No, not at all. I think I'm scared of being rejected. Every time I pick up the keys to go and drive over to his house I start feeling sick, and just don't go."

"Girl, where's your courage? You gotta grab life by the horns, or it'll all slip past you before you know it."

I know she's right. Somehow I've got to drum up the courage to go and face him.

"Promise you'll go and see him."

"OK, I promise."

"Today!"
Really? Shouldn't I build up the courage first?
"Oy, you, today right?"
"OK."

I'm sitting outside Luke's house in Macclesfield, trying to drum up the courage to go and speak to him. Deep inside me I know what the problem is. It's because I haven't told him I love him. I know it, but I've just not wanted to admit it. He probably thinks I'm still not over Roland. Which I so am. I guess I was over Roland years ago, round about the time he admitted to his third affair something inside of me had died. On top of that, in hindsight I think I can safely say although I loved him, it wasn't the love between a wife and her husband. It was more friendship, lovely in the first years, but not complete. More like a jigsaw with three pieces missing. You can still see the picture clearly, but you know it's not right, not perfect. I understand now that I accepted it because I thought it was all I deserved. And if I didn't love completely, I couldn't be rejected and have my heart broken completely.

I'm frightened. My dad deserted me. My mum, my husband and my only other relative died on me. Everyone leaves me, it's like I'm cursed. I don't want to be rejected again. I mean, what is there to love about me anyway? I've not worked a day in my life. I tend to think of myself first before others, there's no getting around that, I know I do. Nana told me once that would be different once I had my own kids. But I'm getting old. Maybe I'm past childbearing age? I'm not rich anymore. What about me would make any man want me?

Right, that's it. I'm off. I switch the engine back on, put the car into gear…

TAP. I glance up to see Luke knocking on the car window. I turn the engine off and unwind the window.

"You coming in then?" he asks.

Well, it'll look silly if I run away. "Yes."

He doesn't wait for me, so I follow him into his house.

It's a delightful semi-detached on quite a steep hill. It's got a lovely cottage vibe going on. It's the kind of house I might have purchased if I hadn't kissed goodbye to my late husband's inheritance.

"Come into the kitchen," he says, as I'm hovering in the hallway. "Coffee?"

"Yes please."

Luke makes us coffee and we sit at the kitchen table.

I wrap my fingers around the cup and wonder how to start.

"Sorry I didn't answer your texts."

"That's OK, you were probably busy."

"Umm."

Come on, Charity, you can do this. "I have something I would like to say to you."

"That's what I thought when I saw you sitting in your car." He grins at me and raises one eyebrow. I feel a portion of our old connection come back.

"I want to explain why I didn't tell you I love you."

"I think that's pretty obvious, no need to explain."

"It's not because I don't love you, Luke."

"No?"

"No." Gosh, he's not making this easy. "Everyone leaves me," I blurt out.

144

"I'm still here."

"Yes for now. But eventually you'll tire of me, and you'll leave me."

"I'm not Roland."

"No, of course not. I'm not saying you're like him."

"Are you sure? Because that's what it sounds like to me."

"Everyone leaves me." It's a sigh of a sentence, a breeze of confession that I'm not worth loving, not forever anyway. That eventually, everyone leaves, including Luke.

Luke scrapes his chair and inches closer, he takes my hands in his. "Look at me."

I look up.

"I'm not *everyone* else, I am me. And I love you, Charity Byron. I'm not planning on ever leaving you. You're like warm socks on a cold day to me."

"What?" I laugh. I can think of more flattering comparisons.

"My Nan knitted me a pair of multi-colored socks when I was little. She told me she'd made every stitch with love, and that it was her love in the making that would always keep me warm. You're like those socks. I loved those socks so much I wore them until I couldn't fit into them anymore. I still have them in my sock drawer, as a keepsake and reminder that my Nan loved me."

Luke reaches up and smooths the hair on my forehead to the side. "I know I've come into your life when you're going through a lot of pain. I knew this wouldn't be easy, but I have loved you for a long time. I can't believe how lucky I am sometimes when I'm holding you. Gosh, Charity the love I have for you is like a furnace inside me."

145

"Oh."

"You have to be brave as I have to be patient. If we do move forward together I know there is a happy ending for us. Will you take a chance on me?"

I nod. I nod again, and again. Like a nodding dog in a car window, up and down, up and down. I throw my arms around Luke's neck, then lean back and gaze into his beautiful warm eyes. "I love you," I say, and then my lips are on his. Life is for living. Fear is the thief of joy, and I refuse to submit to its claws anymore. I will be adventurous. I will live my life. I will be courageous. I will sail the seas and ride out the storms.

Chapter 17

ON JULY 14th MASKS BECAME COMPULSORY. I feel self-conscious as I put on my white face mask and enter the supermarket. In the doorway I stop, spray a cloth generously with antiseptic spray and wipe as much of the trolley down as I can. Sorry, I say in my mind to the people queuing behind me. Better to be safe than sorry.

An uncanny but momentous moment trumpets my entrance as I walk into the set of a science fiction movie. A one-way system is marked by red arrows and barricaded aisle entrances. I can work out how far I've walked around the shop by the two-meter distance yellow stickers on the floor, by the way, the ones that most people seem happy to ignore! The ones that look suspiciously like toxic waste markers! I'm reminded of a sixties film clip I was shown once on YouTube, where they advise you to keep insect spray so you can kill the plethora of flies that will bombard you after a nuclear bomb! I kid you not, not only are the yellow hazard stickers the same but I'm still, after all this time, pondering on how the flies get to survive.

I stretch back as far as my rather stiff spine will allow when some, to be polite let's say… gentleman, leans in front of me to reach some celery. Oh, but my mind is having a heated debate on the things I'd like to say. I have a strong impression that I want to enact a scene from Dirty Dancing when Baby repeats back to Johnny 'this is my dance space, you don't go into mine and I don't go into yours'. I'm playing the whole thing in my mind, swinging my hand out in front of me in a circle. Of course I could never get away with wearing the tiny pink outfit she wears, but hey a girl can dream and I have the little white pumps at least. But back to the point, are these people not watching the news every day? Repeated public announcements tell us, Hands – Face – Space. Come on man, this is only going to go away if we follow the guidelines. After five minutes of an internal rant I ponder on the possibility that I might need to get out more!

Do I tell him what I think? No, of course not, I smile politely and take a step backwards so he can eat his heart out on celery sticks. At least the shelves are stocked again. The manic urge to fill my trolley has thankfully abated. At the tills I overhear one of the staff talking about Little Fires Everywhere and I just have to jump right on in.

"Wasn't it great," I add my pennyworth. Maybe they're used to people desperate to talk because they allow me into their staff inner-circle with welcoming smiles and encouragements to continue. I'm like a runaway train, full steam ahead for not only that program dissection but also another two. Me, the person who doesn't like to talk much, especially to strangers, totally at home and comfortable talking to the ladies who really are becoming like family as I make eye-contact and smile at them each time I come to do my once-per-week shop.

As I drive home the song Hungry Eyes is playing on a loop in my mind. Nothing else for it, tonight I'm going to have to watch it again.

Time slips by. It's not possible to explain what fills the days, or where they go to. Most of the time, I have no idea which day of the week it is. I was most upset yesterday when I'd realized it was Sunday. I only have a rum and coke on Friday and Saturday nights. I have just two each night, but I enjoy them. They are the treat that signifies that it's the end of another week. Somehow I'd gone right through the weekend without realizing it, I felt deprived. Luke burst out laughing when I told him on our daily video call. He rubbed it in by saying he hadn't forgotten it was Friday and had enjoyed a couple of cans! I miss him so much. He hasn't had a day off since going back to work. He says it's great for his bank account. I'm not so sure it's great for our relationship though.

Chapter 18

THURSDAY NOVEMBER 5th, BONFIRE NIGHT and the second Coronavirus lockdown has begun. There's a general atmosphere of doom and gloom. I feel low. The bravado from March has long since dissipated. Gosh, but will this ever be over? I know it's for our sake that we're here again. Still, I wonder if we're doing the right thing. Maybe it would be better for herd immunity to be allowed to develop, get it and get over it? I think of the nurses and doctors, no then they'd never cope, of course it's best to try and keep everyone virus free. Still, the economy, job losses and depression, all are taking a terrible hit. And I don't mean financial depression; I mean the general population depression. Will we ever go back to normal? Does normal even exist anymore? Have our lives changed so much that there will never be a returning to where we were? Is our 'crazy' going to become our children's 'normal'? Are face masks here to stay? Gosh, I hope not. Still, my cold sore was covered up nicely today and no need for makeup... small mercies maybe?

My iPad rings. Picking it up I swipe and accept the incoming video call from Luke. I've been worked up all day. "Did you see the news about the mink farms?"

"Hello love, how you doing?"

Yes, I should probably have started with hello. "Hiya, I'm OK thanks, same-old-same-old, nothing changes. How you doing? Have you got a day off soon?"

"Yes actually, I'm off this weekend. I thought we could go for a walk on Saturday."

"It's forecast to rain."

"Then wear a rain mac." He's laughing at me, but it makes me smile.

"Where shall we meet?"

"Let's go to the reservoir, we can walk for hours around there."

"And keep a two-meter distance."

"Yes, and keep a distance."

"I miss your arms."

Luke bursts out laughing. "I hope you miss more than my arms?"

"Of course I do, but I miss being held. I feel lonely and isolated."

"You should have moved back into my parents before this lockdown hit, you had a week's warning to make up your mind."

"I know, but being cooped indoors for a month with people who are caring, but are however, still relative strangers to me, it just felt a bit…"

"I understand. I would have moved in with you if I didn't have to work. Look, don't get down, it won't last forever and they're getting closer and closer to releasing a vaccine for it."

"To be honest I don't know if I want to take it. Most vaccines take years to be developed and tested before they're rolled out to the public. We don't know what side-effects there might be. It might end up being like 'I Am Legend' with Will Smith, and we'll be killed or worse as the mutated vaccine destroys humankind."

Luke is laughing so much his image is bobbing up and down as his hand shakes.

"You never know!" I pipe indignantly.

"Don't you worry your pretty little head about anything. If zombies become part of our lives, I'll look after you."

"Do you own a gun?"

"No."

"So exactly how do you propose to kill them?"

"I could use a slingshot and pop stones at their heads, or maybe you could sing for them, that would surely kill them." Luke roars.

I'm not amused. "Have you seen today's news?"

Luke takes a moment to compose. "No, I'm fed up of hearing about the US election. The last I heard Trump declared if he doesn't win he's leaving the US. It's just ridiculous."

"I'm really worried, Luke."

"About Trump leaving the country or winning?"

"Neither. Stop joking around for a moment. There are these mink farms in Denmark, and they've got a new mutation of Covid19 and it's jumped to humans. The UK has closed its borders to anyone coming from Denmark. This is serious crazy, Luke. I'm frightened. What if we can't stop this new strain, what if there is nothing left but death for us in the days to come?"

"Oh, sweetheart, slow down. We'll be fine. There have been different strains of these flu-like viruses throughout history. They come and they go, it seems they are part of life. Stop worrying. There is nothing new under the sun."

"I didn't even know there were such things as mink farms, did you? You should see the small cages they're in, it's just awful. The Danish government has confirmed they're going to cull around 15 million mink! That's a crime against nature. What on earth are we doing when we allow 15 million mink to live in cages? I thought fur had been banned years ago. Why are people still wearing it for goodness' sake?"

"I honestly don't know."

By Saturday, November 7th there have been 48,475 deaths attributed to Coronavirus in the UK. As I drive through the relatively empty roads towards the reservoir I can't help the fear that builds up in me all the time. What if what we've seen so far is just the tip of the iceberg? What lies ahead of us? Just death and destruction?

There are only a handful of cars in the parking lot, so it's easy to spot Luke's. I pull up alongside him. I can't help a little chuckle when I notice that the cars are parked in a row with a good two-meters in-between each one, even the cars are social distancing! The sky is dirty grey and depressingly low. It's cold and drizzling. We're only allowed to meet outdoors, so here we are, dressed to the nines in unflattering rain gear.

"Hello you," says Luke smiling at me.

"Hi." I get out of the car and quickly pull my mac hood up over my head; one thing I don't want is to catch a cold of any description right now. I can't imagine doing my weekly shop with the sniffles, or worse a cough! People would look at me like I was a leper. I shuffle my backpack on and lock the car.

"Ready?"

"As I'll ever be." I'm avoiding looking at his face. I just know I'll want to throw myself at him and beg him to hold me if I do.

"Did you see the Iron Man on your way in?"

"Oh, was he made of iron? I thought it looked like wood. Yes, great isn't he?"

"I love the way bits of art are seemingly just dropped into different locations. I had to go and visit the Angel of the North, to see it up close. It's 66 feet tall and made of steel, so impressive."

"I didn't know you liked art?" I had to stop. We were about to hit the foot path that wasn't wide enough for us to walk beside each other, we would have to walk in single file. My hearing is not the greatest and with my hood up I'm never going to hear Luke.

Luke stops too. "I'm not into paintings that much, although I do appreciate them, but I love outdoor art. What about you? What do you like?"

It's a reminder that we really still don't know each other that well. "I love lots of things. Like you I appreciate outdoor sculptures, but what I really love is nature. When I was little I couldn't walk into a wood without wanting to run and hug all the trees. Sometimes when I see a breath-taking view I get frustrated because I can't wrap my arms around it and keep it forever."

"You could take a photo."

"Oh, I do, all the time. I've even got my phone on me now so I can take some. But looking at them later is not the same. They're like echoes, fading images but not the real thing. In fact, before we start, let me take one of you now."

Luke is gracious and poses with the water in the background while I take about twenty different shots. "It'll be time to turn around and come back if we don't get a move on," he says eventually.

"How long will it take us?"

"If you're going to stop and take photos every minute then all day, but otherwise it's about an hour and a half. Five miles circuit all the way round."

Despite the distance we have to cover, I'm loving this walk. The wet blanket sky can't dampen the happiness I feel being with Luke. There's an ease between us that means we talk while continually walking. The hardest thing is not being able to reach up and kiss him, and I can tell by his glances that he feels the same. The footpath takes us around the dam wall and then through farmland, before looping back towards the visitor center. We find the route easy to follow. The terrain is varied, from paved roads to narrow muddy tracks. All in all I feel like I'm an intrepid explorer, *obviously* I know thousands have trodden the path before me, but still a girl can dream.

The autumnal colors are beautiful. The varied shades of green are hard to describe. How blessed we are to live in such a beautiful country. The parking lot has cost us a few pounds for the day, but what a cheap price to pay for such enjoyment. We're nearing the end of the walk. It's gone too quickly. If it had been a dry day we could have sat on the grass for an hour and just talked, but it was way too muddy. The still waters of the reservoir are deep blue and look icy. I know we're approaching the end and I just can't stand it.

Spinning around without warning I look at Luke, who nearly stumbles into me. I'm pleading with my eyes.

155

He understands. He takes a step and is in front of me. He cups his soft, loving hands around my face and leans down. His lips demand mine. His kisses are urgent and full of passion. We kiss. We kiss for so long I don't know how long we've been standing there. A touch of a breeze moves through the trees and the remaining golden leaves rustle, like a round of applause. It is the most passionate kiss we've had. When he finally releases me I wobble and he reaches out to grab me with a gentle laugh.

My eyes flutter open. I've forgotten where we are. I don't want this to end. All I know is that I belong to him, fully and completely.

With lockdown rules broken there is no point in keeping our distance anymore, and Luke takes my hand as we walk the last part.

"Will you move in with me?" I ask once we're back at the cars.

"I can't."

"Why not? I don't live that far away from work?"

"It really isn't that."

"Then what is it?"

"I don't think I can control myself anymore knowing you are in a room next to me. To be honest, I think I would be climbing into your sheets."

"Would that be so bad? I mean we've both been married before, and we're not teenagers anymore."

Luke looks down at his feet for a moment and shoves his hands in his pockets. Suddenly, I'm wondering if the memory of wonderful Tanya prevents him from giving himself fully to me.

"It's OK, sorry. I don't mean to push you." I feel my joy shriveling up.

Luke pulls his hands out of his pockets and takes hold of both of mine. "When the time is right, we will be together fully. Just be a little more patient."

"OK." Well what else can I say? I can't help the rejection volcano from erupting. I mean, maybe he just isn't attracted to me in that way?

"Hey, you." Luke knocks my chin gently with his hand. "I'll call you tomorrow, you going to be alright?"

"Sure, I mean of course."

I pretend to be doing something in my handbag and just offer Luke a quick wave as he drives away. I stop my messing and stare out of the window. Am I not what he wants really? Is he just being nice to me because he knows how horrible Roland had been? I look at myself in the rear view mirror and can't help chuckling. My hair is all ruffled up, my pupils are fully dilated, my cheeks rosy and my lips swollen and bruised deep red. There is no mistaking that I've just been kissed. Tension in me fades a little as I contemplate on the fact that no one kisses like that if they don't like the person. Whatever is going on with Luke, I'm suddenly assured that he both loves and wants me.

On the way home I turn the radio on full and sing my heart out. Life is good. God is good. Thank God for beautiful countryside. Thank God that a handsome, utter dish of a man with a massive heart has fallen in love with me. Thank God!

Just before reaching home as I drive along a road upon which I am the only car, I remember a joke I've seen on Facebook recently. It's one where Wally is standing in an

157

empty street. No need to search for him, there's no one else around! Such are the days in which we're living. These are unprecedented times. But at least we're all in it together, and not just the whole of Great Britain, but the whole of the world. Never has there been such a time when we should be working together.

Where's Wally 2020

Chapter 19

NOVEMBER HAS BEEN PAINFUL, but December has comes with an outpouring of good cheer. Family bubbles can once more be connected. Boris isn't the Christmas Grinch after all! He's a bouncing, all-optimistic Father Christmas. There is an equal amount of argument for both locking us down and for just getting on with it. The government has to balance somewhere in-between the two, searching for the best solution, while borrowing money like it's candy, and plunging us into huge national debt.

Luke is coming around for dinner, and I just feel like all is well with the world once more. I've made slow-cooked beef bourguignon and the house is full of the rich aroma coming from the slow-cooker. I have my favorite red to wash it down with, Châteauneuf-du-Pape.

For the first time since we have been dating I'm super sensitive to what I should wear and look like. I want to look my best for him, but it's a meal at home so I don't want to appear as if I'm setting him up to jump on his bones. He's made his intentions very clear on that point, more's the pity. Lord, you'll have to forgive me; I'm still learning to be a good person.

In the end I opt for jeans and a soft pink blouse. The pale pink is good for my reflection and my hazel eyes deepen against the soft color. I've had my hair up and then down several times, in the end I've gone for the look I feel is more feminine, and my thick, dark brown hair flows free around my face, the slight wave bouncing down around my shoulders. Just a tiny spray of Jean-Paul Gaultier's Classic, a touch of eye-shadow and a layer of mascara, finished off with deep red gloss on my lips, and hey presto I'm ready.

There's just one more thing I need to do. I take off my wedding and engagement rings.

"Thank you for all the wonderful times we had in the beginning Roland. I'm so sorry I wasn't enough to make you happy. I hope you're in Heaven now and surrounded by peace and love. I hope your parents came to take you home." I kiss them, as if kissing Roland for the last time, and put them in a small box which I put in the drawer. Life is moving forward, as it must. Time drags life ever forward, towards the new - whatever that may be.

Gosh, but I'm feeling nervous. Butterflies dance within me each time I think of Luke. You'd think this was our first date.

With Big Ben punctuality, Luke opens the door and yells, "Hello," at 7 pm on the dot.

Despite the fact that we talk every day on the phone, we are never short of things to say. Happy to chat about things from current events to our favorite movies, and a plethora of other things, we rabbit on and on like life-long best friends. I believe I have found my soul mate. One thing Nana used to tell me was this… 'When the first throws of passion fade, friendship endures.' Over and over she had told me to search for my best friend and marry him. Of course I hadn't listened. But then if I had, would I be in this place right now? Would I have met Luke anyway, or did I need to be in the place I was to meet him? Isn't God eternally in control, gently guiding us to where we should be? Maybe the bad and sad have to happen for us to learn and to grow? I don't

160

know. I don't pretend to have any answers; all I know is that since crying in the dining room and pouring my heart out to God I have felt a peace, which quite frankly is worth more than all the gold in the world!

"You're miles away."

"Oh, sorry! What were you saying?"

"Mum and Dad want you to spend Christmas with us. You will, won't you?"

"I'd love to."

"Great. I have to warn you about the presents."

"Warn me?"

"Yep, we don't spend more than £10 on each present we buy. That's the cap."

"That's fine."

"The other thing is, we often make things instead of buying them, just to let you know. You don't have to make things of course."

"OK, thanks for letting me know." So, under £10 and homemade where possible, no engagement ring for me this year then. I smile at Luke… one day, one day.

Chapter 20

SUNDAY DECEMBER 6TH. My birthday and I'm feeling terribly old and past my prime at the ripe old age of 29! I'm at Luke's house. He's in the kitchen finishing the last touches on the dinner, I've had strict instructions to sit on the sofa and drink Champagne, while I watch The Holiday, one of my all-time favorite films. I'm so glad the second lockdown finished before my birthday!

What a difference a year makes! The last twelve months have felt like being inside a barrel as it charges downhill, getting bumped and jolted, and blind to my destination. But here I am soft landing onto a comfy chair with the man I love. It's been a ride I didn't plan, but life is always, totally about the journey. I've struggled with loneliness so much, yet at the same time I've striven to fill myself with thanksgiving. To continually strive forward, being ever watchful for those special moments, that a life-time-album make.

"You ready?"

"I am," I smile as I follow Luke back into the dining room. This is the first meal he's cooked for me and I can see his nerves are shot.

"My lady," says Luke, pulling back the chair for me.

"Why thank you, kind sir."

He shakes open a napkin and drops it onto my lap.

"Thank you." So unnecessary, but oh so sweet.

A row of candles runs down the center of the table, ruby red rose petals are scattered over the white table cloth. Soft music plays in the background. Everything is perfect, and extremely romantic.

Dinner is Scottish salmon, parmentier potatoes, asparagus and hollandaise sauce. It's absolutely divine. Dessert is Baileys crème brûlée.

"Oh my Lord! I think I must be in Heaven, this is a-ma-zing!"

Relief flashes across Luke's face. "Glad you like it."

"Like it? Wow, I don't think I've ever tasted anything so wonderful. This is definitely going to be my number one food-heaven from now on."

I help Luke clear up and fill up the dish-washer. He makes coffee and we go to the front room to relax.

"Do you want to put the film back on?"

"No thanks, I'm happy with the background music and just talking with you."

"In that case, I think it might be time to give you your present."

"Ooo." I sit up straight.

Luke slides his hand under the sofa cushion and brings out a small square box wrapped in pretty paper. "Happy birthday," he says passing it to me.

"Thank you." I reach up and give him a kiss. With slightly trembling hands I take off the paper and open the box. Inside is a beautifully delicate silver cross on a chain. "Oh, I love it. Thank you. Will you put it on for me please?" I hand him the necklace and half turn on the seat.

After he's clasped it on, he bends and kisses the back of my neck. Shivers run up and down me.

"It fits perfectly. Thank you so much, I love it."

"You're welcome. I know it won't compare with other presents you've received, but I remember you saying that you didn't have a cross except for Nana's old one. There seemed to be something in your voice at the time that made me think you'd like one."

"Yes, I did." I turn around on the sofa again so we're facing each other. "Thank you for such a special evening, it's been lovely."

"I know it's not what you're used to, and I wish I could have given you more."

"Don't be silly, this has been the best birthday I've had since... well since I had my eighth birthday."

"Eight?"

"Yes, it was the last birthday I had before my mum died."

"Oh."

"Oh indeed. It was a normal birthday, I had some school friends around, Mum and Nana cooked up a storm of normal birthday treats. We played pin the tail and musical chairs. It was ordinary, but it will forever be special to me. My favorite part was mum doing up the zip to my new birthday dress. I thought I looked like a princess."

"You probably did."

"Money doesn't buy you happiness, Luke. Please don't ever think because I don't have the luxury I used to have that I am unhappy or feeling deprived. I don't feel like that, I honestly feel very lucky right in this moment."

"Drink your coffee, you. It's decaffeinated so you'll still be able to sleep."

We decide to return to the film. I do love Christmas films. I curl up in Luke's arms and we sink into well-being and contentment together as we watch the feel good movie.

"Come on, time for bed." Luke pulls me gently off the sofa and holding my hands leads me upstairs. Outside his spare bedroom we stop. We're both happily tired and our goodnight kiss is short but tender.

Luke has already gone to work the next morning when I wake up. He's left a note in front of the kettle that says I should make myself at home and stay as long as I like. I smile to myself as I make the coffee. I would like to stay, in fact I'd like to stay and never go home, but we're not there yet.

I normally love Christmas shopping, but this year is different. This year I'm getting creative. I'm lucky to live in the countryside with not far to go before I'm in woods.

It's freezing, and I've got tons of layers on to keep warm. The brisk walk into the country also warms me. I have my wicker basket on my arm and secateurs in my pocket. I'm hunting for holly. I've been watching YouTube non-stop, and I'm going to have a go at making Shirley a holly wreath and a centerpiece for the Christmas table.

The walk is invigorating, the air fresh and crisp and by the time I've filled the basket with holly, my nose is red and my toes freezing. I stop off at the florist on the way home to buy some string, green wire and silver glitter spray.

As I come out of the shop the Sally Army band is playing Hark the Herald Angels Sing, and I stop to listen. There is a bill-board explaining that they're not collecting but asking people to make donations on-line, yet another change in our society. Will folk get used to shopping on-line? Is this the end of our high streets? There are about fifteen people in the band, aging from six to sixty by the looks of it. All smartly dressed in their uniform trench coats and peaked service caps with the bright red rim, the younger members are wearing Christmas hats. It's so quintessentially English and I take out my phone to snap a photo and send it to Luke. I wish he was here with me. Still, I will see him tomorrow.

Back home, after the table piece is made I set about putting checkered cloths over the tops of some homemade blackberry jam. All that's left to make is toffee, fudge and biscuits and then I'll be set.

Chapter 21

CHRISTMAS EVE DAWNS COLD AND BRIGHT. It has been years since we had a white Christmas in Cheshire, but looking at the sky, I feel optimistic. It has that heavy grey feel to it, like the clouds are just longing to burst open and drench us with white crystal patterned snow.

The temperature has remained just above freezing for a while now, and Jack Frost has danced upon the world leaving a glistening winter-wonderland. With my hands wrapped around my coffee mug, and my fluffy dressing gown and slippers on I stand at the back door and stare into the garden through the glass. Nana's garden has been touched by a magical frost. The branches of the trees appear like frosted-glass upon trunks that look like blackened sculptures. The tips of the grass are frozen white blades. I'll have to go out and break the ice in the birds' water fountain and put some fresh in for them, and refill all the feeders.

I miss you, Nana. I hope you're having a ball up there with Mum. Sure you are. I can just hear you singing Christmas carols and asking everyone if they want a mince pie, with clotted cream of course. I love you. Little sparks prickle behind my eyes, but today is not a day for crying and I give myself a full-body shake to snap out of it. Today is Christmas Eve and there is still so much to do.

My contribution towards Christmas dinner is a cooked ham. I put it to soak yesterday, and now I need to change the water and bring it to the boil. Into the fresh water I add two bottles of cider, a quartered apple, carrot, onion, celery, a cinnamon stick and a handful of cloves and peppercorns. I'm going to let it simmer for about four hours, and then later I'll finish it in the oven with some honey glaze. Yum, I love home cooked ham.

With the ham simmering it's time to wrap my presents. Still in my pajamas I put Christmas carols on and pour myself a small glass of Baileys with lots of ice in it. It's only 11 am but it is Christmas Eve and wrapping presents with carols playing, and drinking a Baileys is something that Nana and I always did.

"Here's to you, Mum and Nana, Merry Christmas!" I salute them with my glass and take a sip. It's funny I love this drink so much, but I only ever buy it at Christmas, I'm not sure why.

"Little donkey, little donkey on the dusty road." Don't laugh! I'm on my own, no one can hear me. The presents are spread out around me on the floor. To the left, red sparkly paper (which is making a right mess, I have to say, as glitter falls everywhere) and velvet ribbon, oh and tags. Scissors and Sellotape, and I'm set to go.

I've made some vanilla fudge covered in white chocolate for the girls. I've put the fudge on baking paper inside boxes that I've covered with Disney's Frozen pictures. I thought they might like to use the boxes afterwards to keep their knickknacks in. I hope Lisa doesn't mind that I've made them something sweet. I've also made them a Gingerbread House, which is in a box in the kitchen. I had such fun making the white icing and covering it all with tiny sweets.

"Silent night, Holy night." I stop singing and remember Christmas Eve carol services at church with Nana. I used to love the candlelight services, what a terrible shame that people won't be able to attend this year. The thought mars my otherwise enjoyable day. Think I'll have another Baileys. Luke is picking me up after all, so I don't have to worry about driving.

While I'm up, I switch from carols to popular Christmas songs, and I'm singing along at full belt along to Deck the Halls, when I sit back down on the floor to wrap up Luke's present.

It had been hard to pick out a present for Luke that cost under £10 when I so wanted to give him lots of things. Still, we're going to his parents' house so I will go along with their traditions. One night as we watched a feel-good movie called Mi Casa Su Casa, the idea had popped into my head to give Luke a key to my house for Christmas.

On Etsy I'd found a round wooden disk that the shop owner would engrave for you and turn it into a key ring. It was perfect! I'd ordered one straight away getting it engraved with *Mi casa es tu casa.* I'm not an artistic or poetical type of person but I'd been overcome with wanting to write Luke a poem. Searching the Bible for inspiration I'd read 1 Corinthians 13:4-8. The poem only took me fifteen minutes to write, and not being a poet I feel quite chuffed with myself.

Love is patient, love is kind
Longing twists & me to you does bind
Draw near to me, my own sweet dove
And let me rain upon you deepest love

Love does not boast nor envy nor mock
So upon your heart's door let me knock

169

Tis not arrogant nor rude, it never fails
Allow me in your shadow to trail

Love protects, trusts and always hopes
So wrap around me your soul's true ropes
I will love you fair and true
If you're willing, let us start life anew

I've tried to write it as artistically as possible and I wish I could do calligraphy. If lockdown carries on next year maybe I'll take it up as a hobby, as finding a job is kind of impossible with so many companies closing down.

I fold the paper into a small square and wrap it with the key ring, to which I've attached a key. I hope he doesn't think I'm being too forward, but I really want him to know that I'm ready to take this courtship to the next level. I'm committed to him wholeheartedly, if it were a leap year again next year, I think I'd be tempted to propose. Then again that would take the romance out of it. I think I must be a traditionalist at heart.

In the afternoon I honey-roast the ham and pack my bag. Luke is coming for me at four, so all I need to do now is have a shower and I'm all set. Christmas here I come!

Just as I'm getting ready to get in the shower, my cell rings. I run across the room wrapped in a towel to grab it before the caller goes. I don't recognize the number.

"Hello?"

"Hello Charity, this is Shirley."

Oh my Lord, what's happened? "Is everything OK?"

"Yes, yes, all is good. I got your number from Luke. I just wanted to make sure he let you know we dress up on

Christmas Eve and Christmas Day with something Christmassy. It can be anything you like, a t-shirt or jumper with something on it, or just some sort of Christmas earrings. Anything really. I just didn't want you to feel left out and I'm sure Luke would have forgotten to tell you."

Phew, such relief. What a year this has been and my first thought is to assume something bad has happened. I chuckle in relief. "Actually, he did tell me. I'm all set."

"Wonderful! I can't wait for you to get here. We're all massive Christmas fans by the way, I hope you're prepared."

I laugh again. "I love Christmas and all the trimmings. You don't need to worry about me."

"Ahh, that's lovely. OK, Charity I'll let you go. See you soon!"

"See you soon."

I give in to tears when I'm in the shower. It's such a funny thing to have equal amounts of sorrow and happiness bubbling around inside me. I wish Nana was here. I know she would have loved the Smith family as much as I do. I also wish that Roland was still alive. I wouldn't want to still be married to him, but I wish he had lived and found happiness. Yet, mingling with the tears of loss is the overwhelming joy of love and hope. Strange, strange world. Fiercely vibrant with the possibility of happiness, and yet frequently submerged under avalanches of sorrow. I don't understand. It's hard to work through my labyrinth of emotions. I do have peace now because of my renewed faith. I can't imagine how people live without the knowledge that they will meet their loved ones again, now that is sad. Of course I also have Luke. Luke who takes my breath away,

171

who makes me feel loved and cherished like I've never been before. He's my rock.

When Luke knocks on the door I'm ready. Boxes and bags sit in the hallway, laden down with tons of goodies to share.

"Ta da!" I sing as he comes in. "What do you think? Christmassy enough?" I've got dancing, flashing reindeer ears on my head, Christmas stocking earrings dangling from my lobes, but the crème de la crème is my elf outfit, complete with leggings, top and pointed shoes with tinkling bells on their toes.

Luke bursts out laughing. "Well no one can accuse you of not getting into the Christmas spirit. Come here my little elf, and give us a hug."

I throw myself into his outstretched arms. His jumper starts playing We Wish you a Merry Christmas as soon as I lean into his Father Christmas nose.

"Oh, that's great," I say, laughing.

"Nah, come back here you, I've not finished with you."

One of Luke's arms snakes around my waist pulling me close to him. The other hand holds the back of my neck. I'm pinned against his lips, and I've got to say, I'm not complaining. I'm quite happy to spend the whole of Christmas like this. I totter a little when he finally lets me go.

"Merry Christmas Eve, beautiful," he says with a tender smile.

"Merry Christmas Eve, to you too."

Aware that once we arrive we will not be alone again until Boxing Day evening, we take the chance to have a good natter on the way to Stockport.

"Wow, look at that," I say pointing at a house that has every inch of house and garden covered with Christmas decorations.

"There's a competition around here as to who can burn the most electric. We'll be taking the kids for a walk tonight to the Carol Service, and we'll 'decoration hunt' along the way."

"We're going to a Carol Service? I thought the churches were closed?"

"It's not being held in the church this year. It's being held in the shopping center precinct. We'll all be outside and we'll keep our distance from everyone. But we'll be together celebrating the birth of Christ and that's all that matters."

"It sounds wonderful."

The house is noisy and full by the time we get there. Poppy and Rose are running around playing hide-and-seek, Pete and Dave are having a beer in the front room, and Lisa is helping Shirley prepare a buffet tea. After dropping my stuff off in my room I go straight to the kitchen to help the ladies and Luke joins his dad and brother in the front room. The girls want Elf to go and play with them and Shirley shoos me off.

"Tea will be ready soon, you go. They've not got enough time to completely wear you out," laughs Shirley.

Tea is jolly but also quick, no one wants to miss the service or the decoration hunt. We dress up in warm coats, hats, gloves and boots (I take off my elf shoes with regret) and set off for the shopping center. The girls run up and down the pavement eager to be the first to spot the next decorated house first. I literally don't know where they get their energy from; they'll surely sleep well tonight. I'm surprised how packed the town is. It appears like the whole neighborhood has come out for the service, and brought all their dogs with them too. I've never seen so many in one place.

A massive tree towers behind the stand from which the vicar gives his short sermon. The cafés and shops have opened late so that they can sell all sorts of Christmas goodies. The sweet smell of cotton candy rolls over the crowd from a mobile dispenser, toffee apples are being eaten by numerous children, and adults are sipping on hot mulled wine.

People hold up plastic candles as the brass band begins to play. I join in the carols with gusto, despite Luke's reference to my lack of angelic vocal ability... and then it starts snowing.

The girls go crazy, and I know how they feel. It's been years since we had a white Christmas. The flakes are few and very light, but already the roofs are beginning to turn white. Could this Christmas get any better? The good cheer from everyone is intoxicating; lots of people the Smiths know are blowing kisses and good wishes and imitating hugs from two-meters away. Even strangers are smiling and wishing us a Merry Christmas.

On the walk home, Luke and Pete go either side of Dave to support him. He's out of breath and puffing. Shirley had tried to get him to stay at home but he would have none of it.

"Life is for living," he had declared before having a coughing fit.

Back at the house the adults have Baileys as we sit and watch Home Alone with the girls. I'm cozy in the crook of Luke's arm. How I wish I had a family of my own. Please

God, maybe one day you would bless me further and give me children of my own?

Chapter 22

"MERRY CHRISTMAS, BEAUTIFUL!" I can't believe Luke has had to wake me up. I reach up and wrap my arms around his neck.

"Merry Christmas, handsome."

"Come on, get up. You've got to see this." With no decorum he yanks back the duvet, grabs me by the hand and literally drags me out of bed.

"Wooah, what's the hurry?"

"This is," says Luke, pulling back the bedroom curtains.

I can't help but gasp. Everything is white. Happy tears sting my eyes.

"Oh, it's beautiful."

Luke stands behind me and wraps his arms around me, placing his chin on my shoulder. "Not as beautiful as you," he whispers.

I think I could stand here for ages, but suddenly, Poppy and Rose are charging in and run up to us. "Uncle Luke, Uncle Luke, you've got to come. We're not allowed to open our presents until we're all together."

We both laugh. "We're coming girls, we're coming," says Luke, and taking my hand we follow the girls and race down the stairs.

The tree is artificial but it looks so real. Branches thick and fat like they should be, it's bursting to overflowing with multi-colored twinkling fairy-lights and a plethora of ornaments. It looks beautiful. Underneath it is a pile of wrapped presents.

"Here you go, love," says Dave passing me a mug of coffee.

"Oh, thanks, how did you know?"

Dave just chuckles and makes his way to his favorite chair to watch all the shenanigans.

"I don't know which the girls are more excited about, the presents under the tree or the snow outside," laughs Shirley.

"Both!" yell both the girls at the same with a burst of giggles.

"Are you ready, girls?" asks Lisa.

"Yes!" they both squeal.

"OK then, get to it."

They dive under the tree and pull out a present each, check the label and then jump up. Poppy delivers a present to Dave, while Rose delivers one to Luke.

"That's from me," says Rose handing it to Luke. She looks as pleased as punch.

"Ooh, I can't wait to open it," says Luke holding it to his chest.

The girls deliver all the presents to everyone and then we open them at the same time. I'm speechless at the thought and effort that has gone into my special presents, and I watch eagerly to see that everyone likes the presents that I made for them.

Shirley has made me an apron. It's a proper old-fashioned bib and skirt, and she's embroidered daisies along the edges.

"Oh my goodness, I love it," I say, getting up and giving her a hug.

"That's so Luke can tie your apron strings to the kitchen table," laughs Pete.

"Hey!" pipes up Lisa, swiping at his arm.

"Well you know the way to a man's heart is through his stomach," chuckles Dave.

"Which, although it's politically incorrect, is quite near the truth," laughs Shirley, "especially in your case!" She throws a scrunched up piece of paper at him.

Luke has saved my present to open last, and I hold my breath as he undoes the wrapping. He looks at the key and turns to me with a smile. Then he opens the paper and reads the poem. I hope it's not too pushy. It's obvious from the last line and the present of a key that I am asking him to move in with me again, but what will he think.

His face is expressionless. I can't tell what he's thinking. Oh my goodness, he doesn't like it! I feel sick. It's too pushy, too much. After all, he's made it clear he wasn't ready to get serious. Stupid silly woman, what have I done? He stands up. Gosh he's going to go out of the room he's so embarrassed. Oh no.

But instead of leaving the room, Luke drops to one knee in front of me.

"I know our tradition is only £10 presents allowed, but I spoke with Mum and Dad and they agreed there could be an exception to the rule." Luke puts his hand in his dressing gown pocket and pulls out a small red box. He lifts the lid and presents to me the most beautiful diamond ring.

I gasp. The girls clap.

"Charity, will you do me the honor of becoming my wife?"

I can't talk. My chin is wobbling like crazy. My eyes are spilling over with tears. Luke looks at me questioningly.

"Yes," I manage to whisper. "Yes, and a hundred times yes."

Everyone laughs and claps. Luke slips the ring onto my finger and then draws me to my feet. He gives me a soft kiss and then we're hugging. Everyone is clamoring to hug and congratulate us.

"Let's see, let's see," cry the girls.

I turn around and show them the ring. "Ooo," they say in unison.

After some home-baked croissants for breakfast, the ladies prepare the dinner, while the men play board games with the girls. All the time Christmas music is playing in the background.

At three o'clock we gather around the dining table for dinner. The table looks festive and merry. Pulling Christmas-crackers are on each plate; the center-piece made from holly sits around a row of thick red candles which have been lit. The room diffuser is emitting the aroma of cinnamon and orange. Once all the food has been placed on the table and we've sat down, Dave holds out his hands. One by one we join hands and close our eyes.

"Dear Lord above, how great Thou art. How merciful and loving. We thank you for the roof over our heads, for the clothes on our backs and this wonderful abundance of food on our table. Lord, 2020 has been a trying year. With floods, fires, shootings and Covid as well, it has sometimes felt like the end-times have come. Whether they have or they haven't is not relevant to us, dear God. For your Son came down and spilled His blood for us. How truly grateful are we, that our sin has been wiped away by His sacrifice so that our forever home will be with You in Heaven. Thank you

God, for the National Health Service, and for the wonderful people who go out of their way to help others.

"As we move into 2021 Lord, help us to be better people. Help us to appreciate each and every moment of life we have. May our hearts be full of worship and thanksgiving. And may we never forget that You never leave nor forsake us, no matter how hard the times are.

"With thanks we say…"

"Amen," says everyone.

The day has been one of the most precious days of my life. Now that we're engaged, Luke has decided we can sleep together. Sleep only mind, as we are in his parents' house. We're thinking of a spring wedding, something low key but special. Luke is snoring gently in my ear. His arm is wrapped tight around my waist. I feel loved and wanted. How exceptional is that? Besides my Mum and Nana, I have never felt love like this. He knows me inside and out and still wants me! My heart has become like a sponge, totally squishy and oozing joy. I promise to love this man always, God. I will do my very best to make him happy. Thank you God, thank you so much, for bringing me out of the mire and putting my feet on solid ground. Thank you for surrounding me with love and a new family. Thank you as well for Megan and Jack, and for all the ventures we have planned for next year, especially for the Wales project Lord, I just know that is going to bless so many people.

I don't know for sure what 2021 will bring, but I do know I'm not alone. Whatever happens we will face it together and be strong.

THE END

If you enjoyed Charity's story could I please encourage you to leave me a review? Without reviews a book never succeeds and I would really appreciate your endorsement and support. Many thanks.

Ecclesiastes 1:9 (New International Version)
[9] What has been will be again,
what has been done will be done again;
there is nothing new under the sun.

Thank you so much for reading

If you'd like to know more about my books please check out my web. http://www.tntraynor.uk

If you enjoyed this book you might also enjoy one of my other books.

Grace in Mombasa
Inspired by the life of Moira Smith.
https://www.amazon.com/dp/B07KT8S4N7

Faith in Abertillery
Inspired by the Welsh Revival of 1904/1905
https://www.amazon.com/dp/B07VTRJ5T1

A letter from the Author

Dear Readers
Throughout this sadness that is Coronavirus I have wept in
fear that I might not see my sons again. After nine months, I
am still instantly brought to tears at just the hint that I might
never see them again. One lives in Australia, another in the
USA. Whilst two other sons live in the UK, one has an 'at
risk' girlfriend and therefore to protect her, he remains at
home and I haven't seen him in almost a year. My other son
I am so grateful to say, lives not too far away and I see him
when lockdown rules permit. It is hard sometimes to stop
fear from stifling all my joy. I strive to look for the good
going on around me. I wish I was stronger.
It gives me small comfort to look at the past. The Spanish
Flu naturally ran its course in two years, simply fading away.
This pandemic too, shall pass.
Let us pray and hope that the things we have learned about
caring for our neighbors and the world in which we live may
bear fruit and remain long into the future.
My love and prayers are sent to all of you, especially if like
me you have felt the sadness of isolation, or worse, like
Charity, you have lost someone close to you, I send you much
love and heart-felt condolences.
God bless, now and always.
Tracy

Captain Tom Moore

In unprecedented times…
Captain Tom became a symbol of all that is good in
humanity.

Born 30 Apr 1920
100 years old when he walked for the NHS
Knighted on 17 July 2020

What a man! What a marvelous veteran
So inspiring, his task of walking
Put me to shame, my sofa adoring
Stalwart, his spirit in century old frame
Hearing fading, determination blazing
Could I so selfless be? Let's see.
Thank you, Captain Tom
For raising thirty-two mill-i-on!

by T N Traynor
October 2020

Unprecedented times,

But… we *are* in this together!

From the Spanish Flu in 1918, to Coronavirus 2020
Then and now… thank you to our wonderful nurses and
doctors

Here's to 2021! May God abundantly bless you, and
your household.

Printed in Great Britain
by Amazon